A Blazing Dance

A Dicey Dance Series
Book 3

LAUREN MARIE

Excerpt from A Blazing Dance

When he rounded the corner into the lunchroom, he saw Jonah sitting at a table. "Hey, kid. Are you ready for a rematch?"

"Yeah." Jonah nodded but didn't smile.

"Since you won the last game yesterday, I think you start."

The boy made the first move on the checker board. "Mr. Hejazi, are you a mercenary?"

"No, I'm not."

"Sir, yesterday you said you weren't a cop, but that you did security."

"That's right." Hejazi sat back in his chair and watched the boy.

"Can I hire you?"

A BLAZING DANCE

Dedication

To my Papa and Grammy – Ray and Florence Davis. I miss and love you still to this day and know one day we'll meet again.

Thank you to Jennifer Conner and Books to Go, Now. Your support is wonderful.

Thank you to Grace Augustine. Love you, too.

Chapter One

Jarrah Hejazi watched the crowd gathered around his latest client, singer Veronda. His group was hired, at a very good price, six months ago to protect her from screaming fans. He felt glad this was the last stop. As soon as she finished her stage show, he and his team would be free. They needed the break and he was ready to just guard his usual clients. This assignment, of a young singer, was outside his groups' range of experience.

The younger men on his team liked Veronda's music. He hated to act like an old-fogey, but her tunes were not his favorite. The drums were too loud and half the time he couldn't understand the words coming from her mouth.

As he watched the audience something caught his eye. In two different locations he saw a couple of teenagers who weren't watching the concert. He could tell they were stalking the other audience members. They'd move around and then clear a way to another group of people. He knew exactly what they were up to and watched the team of pick-pockets go from group to group.

"Hey, Chief."

Hejazi cupped his hand over his ear. "I can barely hear you. Speak up."

"This is Griggs. Me and Rand think we've got a team of pick-pockets over here."

"Yeah. I've been watching them at this end, too. I'll report it to the house security, but we stay on Veronda."

"Roger, that."

Hejazi continued to watch the crowd and saw another kid reach into a woman's purse. He shook his head. His team had worked continuous jobs for the last two years. He was tired and needed a change of scenery, so did his crew.

Hejazi walked to his personal vehicle and pulled out a handful of envelopes. He went back to his men and handed out bonus checks.

"Okay, guys. We've got a month until we go with Senator Roberts in September, so have a great vacation. We'll meet up in Los Angeles for the briefing."

He guided his SUV south on I-5 straight to Stockton. He'd wanted to stop by Safe Haven and see how things were progressing since it opened eight months ago.

When he parked, he looked up at the huge building. There were many changes and he could tell the non-profit was doing well. Hejazi walked through the gates, up the front steps, and into the main lobby. A tall, dark haired woman came out of an office and stood behind the counter. He hadn't met her the last time he'd visited.

"Can I help you?" she said.

The woman's brown hair floated around her shoulders. There were enough gold highlights to make her light green eyes sparkle. He looked at her stance and could see a chain around her neck. The outline of dog tags pressed against the T-shirt she wore. His interest heightened.

He walked up to the counter and smiled. "Yeah, is Mrs. Black around?"

"Yep, she's upstairs. Can I let her know who you are?"

His eyebrows folded together. "We're you Army?"

"No, Marines." She smiled. "You aren't Jarrah Hejazi, are you?"

"Yes, I am."

The woman nodded. "Rae talks about you. I'm Grace McKay." She walked from behind the desk. "Follow me."

They went to a stairwell and started up.

"How long did you serve, Miss McKay?"

"Call me Grace, please. I was in for twelve years, sir. How about you?"

"The same, twelve years."

"Then you were a secret agent?" She smiled over her shoulder.

Hejazi laughed. "No, Secret Service. I was assigned to a team that protected the secretary of state."

"Impressive."

"Not really, I only did that for a year before I started my own security group. What's your job here?"

"Security."

"Oh." A weird feeling hit him.

"Don't tell anyone though. The kids think I'm a receptionist and part-time cook."

"Your secret is safe with me."

They walked through a set of double swinging doors and entered a huge lunchroom. Windows wrapped around the whole room, letting in light and giving it a warm feel.

Hejazi saw Rae Black at some tables that were moved together and she spoke to a group of kids. He stood by a wall and listened to her. Her belly looked like she hid a basketball under her shirt. He'd heard she and Turner were expecting.

"I'm curious if any of you would be interested in taking some classes?" she asked and the kids groaned. "I'm not talking about math and English. I thought maybe self-defense or cooking?"

"I could be Jackie Chan," one boy said. He made a funny noise in his throat and flexed non-existent muscles.

"Right. Can I get a show of hands? How many

can I count on to show up if I arranged self-defense classes?" Several hands went up. "How about cooking?" A few other hands raised. "Okay, once I get it arranged I'll put a signup sheet on the bulletin board downstairs. If you haven't eaten lunch go for it. Ladies, I'll meet you for dance class in an hour. Mr. Jenkins has appointments with a couple of you this afternoon, don't be late. And Ian, Dr. Johnson moved your appointment to three-thirty. He wants to see how your lungs are doing."

The group broke up and Rae walked toward Hejazi with a grin on her face. "Jarrah, how good to see you." She lifted on her toes and gave him a hug.

"It's good to see you, too, Mrs. Black." He put a hand on her stomach. "I heard about this little one. How soon are you due?"

"It's just a couple more weeks. Turner's gone into insane-father-mode. He doesn't want me working, but I get bored sitting around at home. Daytime TV sucks."

"You said it."

"Can I get you a cup of tea, Rae?" Grace asked.

"That would be great."

"Mr. Hejazi, coffee or tea?"

Asking for a coffee, he and Rae sat at a table. He saw a kid sitting by a window and staring into the sunlight. The kid was small, with light brown hair and wore the saddest look on his face.

Grace brought them the coffee and tea and then left the room. He watched her walk out the door and liked the way she moved.

"Jarrah, what can I do for you today?"

"Nothing really. I was up in Sacramento with a job and thought I'd stop in on my way south. I wanted to see how things were going."

"So far, so good. We have eight, nine kids staying with us full time and about ten others that come and go. We've only needed to turn one away in the last six months but helped him find another place that helps with drug issues. Things are progressing."

"I heard you talking about self defense. Do you need any help?"

"What? Don't you have a job right now?"

Hejazi laughed. "No, the group's taking the next month off and I have some extra time."

"I would definitely take you up on that offer. Do you need a place to stay? Turner and I have plenty of room."

"No, I can find a hotel to crash. Your house is too far out of town." He looked around and saw that same boy sitting by himself. "Who's that kid over there?"

Rae looked to where he pointed. "That's Kit. He won't tell us his real name or where he came from. We've tried to identify him but can't find out anything. He says he's thirteen years old, but I wonder."

"Huh." He looked at her and saw Grace come back into the room. "Do you have a checkerboard?"

Rae frowned. "Yeah, we have a checkerboard in the game room. Hey Grace?"

The tall woman came over to the table and Rae asked her to get the game. "What are you thinking, Jarrah?"

He watched the tall woman walk away and admired her strut. It was part Marine, part regular woman and the more he watched her move the more he wanted to get to know her.

"Hejazi?"

He heard Rae's voice and looked at her.

"I asked you a question," she said. She looked at the door Grace went through. "Can you stay and have dinner with us tonight? I could ask Grace to join us."

"Sure, it would be nice to see Mr. Black."

Grace came up to the table with a cardboard box. She handed it to him.

"Thank you." He stood and went to the table were the boy sat. "Hi. My name's Jarrah Hejazi. Do you play checkers?"

The kid looked up at him with true puppy-brown eyes. "Sure."

He sat down and started to set up the board. "Do you have a name?"

"I'm Kit."

"Hi, Kit. Your move."

Chapter Two

Grace came back up the stairs two hours later and saw Mr. Hejazi and Kit were still involved with the game. They didn't seem to talk much but made the moves on the board.

She found the tall security-man with broad shoulders and muscular thighs attractive. His dark hair and eyes gave him a mysterious look and she hoped he'd be around for a while.

Rae Black walked up next to her. "They've been playing for two hours."

"I wonder if Kit's told him anything."

"Beats me. Why don't you plan on having dinner with us tonight?" Rae put her hand around Grace's arm.

"Are you sure? I wouldn't want to be in the way with your friend."

"Sweetie, Hejazi has two looks he gets in his eyes and on his face. It's either a sympathy look when you cry on his shoulder or he's trying to figure something out for his work. When he looked at you, I saw a third look."

"He looked at me?" Grace said.

"Yes, and you looked at him the same way."

She felt heat in her face and knew she'd turned

red as a tomato. "I need to get back downstairs."

"Wait a minute, here he comes."

Grace turned and saw Hejazi walk toward them. He carried himself with such confidence and strength.

"How did you fair, Jarrah?" Rae asked.

"The kid beat me twenty out of thirty games." He looked over his shoulder. "I have some information."

Grace followed them out of the room and down a hallway toward the offices.

He stopped and lowered his voice. "His name is Jonah Sullivan and he's eleven years old. He has a brother named Jacob who's fourteen. They were dumped at a park and ride in Reno by their mother and after they lived on the street for a few days met some guy named Feathertop who brought them to Sacramento."

"Unbelievable, the kid's been with us for six weeks and all we knew was his nickname." Rae shook her head.

"I've heard of Feathertop. He's sort of like Fagin in Oliver Twist. He promises them food, and safety, and in exchange, they're taught to pick pockets, steal purses, and I've even heard they've robbed some houses," Grace said.

"I was over in Sacramento earlier and think I may have seen his crew. We were protecting the singer Veronda and I don't know how many worked the crowd, but they were good."

"Let me see what I can find out about Jonah

Sullivan." Rae looked toward her office.

"It's sad. I mean, to be dumped by your mom and then his brother brought him here and told him to wait until he came back." Hejazi shook his head.

Grace now found she admired this man's heart. He felt for Kit.

"Turner will be here to pick me up around five o'clock, oh and Grace will be joining us." Rae grinned.

"Great, I won't be a third wheel." He smiled at her.

Grace stared at his dark eyes and realized she couldn't determine what color they were, black or dark brown, but either way, they mesmerized her. When she became aware that he was staring at her, she blushed.

"Rae, could I ride with you and Mr. Black?" she asked.

"You could ride with me. I don't know my way around here and you can direct me," Hejazi said before Rae could answer.

Grace smiled. "Sounds good."

"I should go find a place to stay the night. How about I meet you out front at five o'clock?"

****

Hejazi found a Holiday Inn and booked the room for the next two weeks. He wanted to spend some more time with that kid, Jonah, and see what he could find out about Feathertop. He also wanted to get to know Grace McKay. He smiled at the hotel attendant and took the key, anxious to get to his room.

It had been over ten years since his last date. When he was nineteen, on his first tour of duty, he'd gone home to Chicago for two weeks leave, and his high school girlfriend acted strangely. After a couple of days, she'd told him that she'd fallen in love with an insurance salesman. The news kicked him in the gut and he'd decided to put his time and energy into the Marine Corps, which he did for twelve years and then started his security group. He never wanted to feel his heart tear in half again.

Twenty years passed quickly and this coming October he'd turn forty years old. His business was pretty self-sufficient. He could monitor the security teams wherever he decided to live. He trusted his men and didn't need to be present all the time.

Grace McKay was a beautiful woman and ex-military which gave them something in common. Her height caught his attention, too. His six-foot-five build made it difficult to date smaller women. The fleeting thought that he wouldn't have to bend at the waist to kiss Grace made him smile while he shaved.

He looked at himself in the mirror. "You're putting your cart way before your horse, asshole. She's probably married," he said to his reflection. "Or she's involved with someone and you won't have a chance."

Opening his duffle bag, he pulled out a clean pair of khaki pants, a regular button down shirt, and a brown jacket. He only had two pair of shoes - black work boots and running shoes. He stared at the shoes and thought life on the road had become hell. He grabbed the running shoes.

****

Grace stood on the step outside the Safe Haven building. She wished she had something other than her work jeans to wear to dinner. She'd decided to keep her hair down and one of the teenage girls that stayed at Haven lent her some make-up. Then she found a blouse in the clothes donated to Haven. It was the best she could do.

A black Bronco came down the street and stopped in front of the building. The passenger window rolled down and she saw Hejazi wave at her.

Her heart skipped a beat as she started toward the door. Without her even noticing, he was at her side and opening the passenger door.

"Milady, your carriage awaits," he said and bowed.

Laughing, she got in and buckled up. When he was in his seat, she looked at him and shook her head.

"Man, you are quiet on your feet." She couldn't believe for a man his size he could move with complete silence.

"Oh right." He laughed. "I should turn off the stealth mode for the evening."

She laughed with him and he pulled out onto the road.

"Where are we going?" he asked.

"Sorry, there's a pub over on Pacific Avenue. If

you turn around and head south, this street, Thornton, turns..."

"Into Pacific?" he finished her sentence. "I think I remember that from when Safe Haven was just getting started. How long have you worked there?"

"Almost six months."

"How long have you been out of the Marines?"

"A year and a couple of months."

"How come you still wear your tags?"

That question surprised her and she didn't have a good answer. "I don't have any nice jewelry to wear."

"Sorry, I didn't mean to go into twenty questions. I have to re-learn how to interact with people sometimes. I've spent too much time lately in work mode."

"It's not a problem. We'll get you a beer and some Haggis and you'll be just fine."

"Yuck, Haggis." He stuck out his tongue. "I'd rather have blood stew."

"That sucks, too. You know if it's not cooked right you can get e-coli from it?"

"But if it's cooked right it's not too bad." He smirked.

"Have you cooked it before?"

"Naw, I'm lucky to be able to microwave Mac and cheese. I tend to be a boy in the kitchen."

"Rae is thinking about offering cooking classes."

As he pulled into the parking lot of the pub and stopped, he smiled at her again. "I can make coffee and other things if a qualified cook is giving directions."

"I was joking about the Haggis," she said as she slid off the seat.

Hejazi shut the door and put her hand around his arm. She looked at him and her heart rate doubled. His hand felt warm. They locked eyes and she wanted to say something, but her tongue became thick.

"Miss McKay, I haven't asked anyone out for a long time, but after we have dinner, would you be interested in going to a movie or something?" he asked.

"Or something, yes," she said quietly and smiled. She let him lead the way.

****

When they walked into the pub, Hejazi's heart raced. The woman on his arm was gorgeous and she seemed to like holding onto him. When they walked toward the table where Rae and Turner sat, they bumped hips and he realized their legs were close to the same length.

Hejazi pulled out a chair and seated Grace and then shook hands with Turner. They exchanged pleasantries and he needed to remember not to chow down like he usually did at meals. Since he and his men were always up and running they joked about the three-minute-meal. And, as much as he wanted to just be with Grace, he knew he needed to be patient. This was not one of those times when he could move fast to achieve an outcome. He was in a social setting and needed to behave.

"Rae, I spoke with Sara Ramsey recently. She let me know about your pregnancy. She and Pat are talking marriage. Have you heard anything more from her?" Hejazi asked.

Rae looked at Grace. "Sara and I used to room together."

"She was the one who was injured in the explosion?" Grace picked up her drink and took a sip.

"Yes, and yes, Jarrah, she is making all sorts of plans. I'm surprised Pat hasn't said anything."

"He was assigned to a different team for a few months. I haven't seen him."

"The wedding will be in the fall, so you better let him have the time off." Rae gave him a stern look.

"Hejazi, I understand you were able to get some information from Kit today. Thank you," Turner said.

"You're welcome. I plan on playing checkers with him tomorrow. I want to find out more about his brother."

"We've started to run a search on them, but it could take some time. See if you can get their mother's first name." Turner took a swallow of his beer.

"Why the delay?" Rae asked.

"If the mother dumped them off, I doubt she reported them missing to any authorities."

"God, that's sad," Grace said.

Hejazi reached over to her hand and gave it a squeeze. When he realized what he'd done, he froze and looked at her. Grace smiled and laced her fingers through his. He then found Turner and Rae watched them.

"If you'd like, I could contact my FBI connection and see if they can turn up anything. I'd like to have this Feathertop looked into," Hejazi said.

"I don't think he's into childcare at all. From what I've heard from some of the other kids, the place where they're kept is bad." Grace squeezed his hand.

Hejazi knew exactly how he'd handle the boy tomorrow and see where it took them.

Chapter Three

Dinner only lasted an hour and a half. Rae being eight and a half months pregnant got tired early and said something about swollen ankles.

Hejazi didn't want to say *goodnight*. His plan was getting derailed when Grace got up to leave with Rae and Turner.

"I could always give you a ride back to Safe Haven," he said and stood.

"We're going to run her home, Hejazi. It's on our way," Turner said and helped Rae stand up from her chair.

Grace smiled up at him and put her hand on his arm. "I don't have my car at work. I ride the bus to and from," she said.

"No problem, we can finish our coffee and I can get you home." He felt desperate and wanted to spend more time with her this evening.

She turned back to Turner and Rae. "I would like to finish my coffee."

Rae grabbed Turner's hand and pulled him away.

"We'll see you tomorrow then," she said over her shoulder.

Hejazi heard her tell Turner she'd explain in the car. He sat back down and they stared across the corner of the table at each other.

She leaned forward. "Jarrah, correct me if I'm wrong, but I think we mutually find each other attractive."

He tried to smile. He stood and moved his chair closer to her. They leaned toward one another like two spies working on a conspiracy. Looking into her beautiful eyes, he said, "Grace, I haven't dated for many years. Between my military service and getting my company up and running, I just didn't have the time. I don't want you to think I'm some kind of weirdo, but I'm not certain what's PC with dating anymore."

"Can I ask why you quit dating and how long it's been?"

"When I first went into the service, I was with a woman I'd been involved with since high school. After boot camp, I went to Kuwait for six months. I had a two-week leave, went home, and found she'd fallen for some other guy. They were engaged."

"And you've been with no one since then?"

"Not seriously. I've had a handful of one night stands, but I've never met anyone or saw signs in someone that I wanted to be with."

"Signs? Do you mean auras or something?"

"No, nothing like that. It's just intuition. When I first saw you this morning, I got a feeling that I wanted...no, that I needed to know you. And I don't want you to think I'm blowing smoke. I do want to know you."

Grace smiled and touched his hand. "I don't think you're blowing anything, Jarrah. As crazy as it sounds, I experienced the same feeling. Maybe our moons are in alignment."

"Are you married or involved with someone?" he asked.

"No. I'm single."

It took a second for what she'd said to register in his brain and he started to laugh. His nerves came down to almost normal. "Is it correct to still open doors for ladies or is it considered passé?"

"My own personal opinion is that it's a gentlemanly thing to do. Jarrah, how about we get out of here and go watch the sunset or something. There's a park a mile from here and we could walk along the San Joaquin River."

"That sounds great." He stood and held his hand out to her.

****

They followed a trail along the river. It was a pleasant summer evening. Their hands linked occasionally and they even put their arms around each other's waist.

Grace felt very comfortable with Hejazi. He

25

laughed and spoke quietly about his past and the days he'd been a Marine.

"I was in the service during nine-eleven. The people I work with knew me in those days and it bugs them when I get the stink eye from someone. My grandparents were born in Iraq and came over just after they married sometime in the late 1950's. My mother and father were both born here in the States."

"Are you Muslim?"

"No, what about you?"

"Catholic. My dad's family came from Ireland during the potato famine. My mom's came from Spain. Both sides were Catholic and how they all wound up in Oregon is beyond me. I was born in Salem."

"Are you folks still alive?"

"Yeah, what about you?" She turned toward a small wooden dock and they went down the steps.

"Yep, they still live in the same house outside Chicago. Do you think your parents might have issues with you dating a man with a Middle Eastern heritage?"

"No, I'm a fallen Catholic. The black sheep of the family. I quit the church on my first tour. When I was stationed in Afghanistan, the scariest things were the kid-suicide bombers. I couldn't figure out what God was thinking with all of that and quit going."

"Yeah, that was scary shit."

"After twelve years why didn't you re-up?" She saw him look at her and wished she hadn't asked that question. "I'm sorry, it's not my business."

"No, it's all right. I never intended to do a second tour, but after my girlfriend, I didn't know what else to do. It was what I knew at the time."

She stopped at the end of the dock and leaned on a metal railing. "I did a second tour because I'd been led to believe I was a perfect candidate for Special Ops. I passed the tests and then they checked my eyesight. I wear contacts. That did it and I washed out." She smiled. "Ack...water under the bridge, right? I moped for about six months and then finished my final tour and came home."

She felt his hand move around her waist. There wasn't a thing about Hejazi she didn't find amazing. He was tall, but she didn't have to arch her neck to look at his eyes, and from the brief time she'd put her hand around his waist, she could tell he was muscular.

His hand moved to her cheek and his index finger touched her lips. When his lips covered hers, all she wanted was his tongue touching hers. The pressure on her lips increased as his tongue swooped into her mouth and tangled with hers. As she sucked his lips, she felt his head pop up.

"Grace, I'm a bit out of practice here and hope that I haven't gone overboard. Do you mind tongue?" he asked.

She could tell he was partly serious. "Oh yeah, tongue is a must and you don't seem out of practice."

He wrapped his arms around her and covered her mouth. She could tell he tried to be gentle, but knew he had force and held it back. She wanted it.

Warmth sizzled through her body and she pressed her breasts against his chest. Her hands moved off his shoulders and into his hair as he sucked her tongue and lips. When he pulled back they both were out of breath. He held her close and put his forehead against hers.

"You know what else caught my attention about you this morning, Miss McKay?"

"What was that?" She looked into his eyes.

"Your incredible height and long legs."

"Please, God, don't call me an Amazonian. I might have to hate you forever."

"I wasn't going to say that. I like your height, for selfish reasons. I don't have to bend at the waist to kiss you and our bodies match up perfectly." He put his hands on her hips and pulled her against him.

"Why, Mr. Hejazi, I think you're happy feeling me up," she said and shimmied her hips against him.

His hands moved down to her butt and pinched her cheeks. "Man, if that isn't an understatement. I almost had a heart attack when Turner offered to drive you home. I wasn't near ready to say goodnight."

She smiled at him and touched his lips again. "Jarrah, do you have a condom?"

He stared at her a bit shocked, and after a second, shook his head. "I didn't think there was a chance of anything happening this evening."

"I think your chances are very good, just not tonight. I *am* on the pill, but like the extra security when I first meet someone."

"That makes perfect sense."

"We'll get it sorted out tomorrow, okay?"

"It's a date." He kissed her again.

"You know, I'm reluctant to say this, because I could stand here all night with your arms around me, but I do need to get home. I have to be at work at seven o'clock tomorrow." She frowned.

"You're being the responsible adult."

"I suppose."

His hand moved through her hair and he licked her top lip. "I like the responsible adult very much. She's an incredible kisser."

"She likes you, too."

They hugged each other and then walked hand in hand back to the Bronco. As he drove her to her apartment, she kept glancing at him and couldn't believe how this evening turned out.

Chapter Four

Hejazi stood in the hotel bathroom with a towel wrapped around his waist. He shaved, again, and thought the last time he'd shaved two days in a row was when his sister got married. He did the math and it would be five years in September.

"You are such an ass," he mumbled at himself. He wanted to look his best for Grace. "And what would she think if you didn't shave? That you are scruffy and don't take care of yourself, maybe." He frowned at his reflection. "If the men could see you now they'd give you shit until next Christmas. Straighten up."

After he'd dropped Grace off at her apartment, he'd spent the next couple of hours thinking about her. Every time he remembered the kisses they'd shared his shaft twitched and he'd needed to jack off twice. She was a beauty, but he wanted to take his time.

Once dressed, he jumped into the Bronco and headed to Safe Haven. A big burley man sat at the front desk and looked at Hejazi as he walked into the lobby.

"Can I help you?" he said in a deep bass voice.

"Yeah. Where can I find Grace McKay?"

"She's up on the fourth floor in the kitchen. Just follow the loud music."

Hejazi took the stairs two at a time and up on the fourth floor heard a pounding beat. When he turned into the kitchen, he stopped and knew he was in trouble. Grace and three other girls stood with their backs to the door. They were working on some kind of dough and all four shimmied their hips and sang along with the song. He couldn't take his eyes off Grace's curvy ass. He leaned against the doorway, hypnotized. The young girl on the end turned to grab something off the island and spotted him.

"Miss McKay, we have a guest," she said.

Grace looked over her shoulder and smiled at him. "Good morning, Jarrah."

He nodded but couldn't think of an appropriate thing to say. *I want to screw your lights out* - didn't seem like the right thing.

She washed her hands and dried them on a hand towel hanging from the pocket of her jeans. "I'll be right back. Don't start the fryer yet." When she walked up to him, she took his hand and pulled him down a hall. She opened a door into an empty room and once they were in, pushed it closed and pressed the lock.

They stared at each other, causing warmth to flood his system.

"I had the best dream about you last night, but I don't think I was really asleep. I got very wound up and..."—she smiled at him—"well, I got wound up."

Hejazi walked up to her and framed her face with his hands. "I think I had the same dreams and got wound up twice." He placed his lips on hers and felt her hands on his waist. Their tongues twirled together and he thought if they continued, they wouldn't leave the room for a while.

"Jarrah," she whispered and continued to kiss his mouth. "If we don't stop, I'm going to peel off my clothes. I want you so badly, but I have to help with the apple fritters."

He kissed her one more time and pulled back holding onto her upper arms. "I'm going to love getting to know you. And,"—he moved closer—"you have a great ass. Watching you dance just now has wound up again."

"Same here. I'm hot for you and can feel you against my stomach." She opened her eyes and a crease formed between her eyebrows. "Did I just say that out loud?"

Hejazi laughed. "Yep, you were brave enough to say it."

Her grin got bigger and her eyes smiled, too. "I wanted to say some gritty things last night but didn't want you to think I was a slut."

"The only way I'd think that, is if you screwed the whole first division at Camp Pendleton."

She hugged him and continued to laugh. "Not likely to happen. It would hurt too much. I thought you said you were out of practice."

"Just a little. Okay, serious time. Where can I find Kit?"

"He's in the lunchroom with the checkerboard all set."

"Has he waited long? I told him I wouldn't be back until after ten."

"Since about nine o'clock. Jarrah, he's been sitting in that same spot for a couple of weeks waiting for his brother. I don't think he's waiting just for you."

They walked back down the hall. "Will you stay for lunch?" she asked.

"I'd like that."

"We got three crates of apples from Gavin Zylstra up in Seattle. We're using the Granny Smiths for pies and apple fritters. Do you like them?"

"I knew I was in trouble. I may eat all the fritters." He stopped in the hallway and touched her cheek. "Can you get off earlier than five o'clock if needed?"

"Possibly."

"Good." He started to turn and then grinned at her. "We'll have dinner after."

"After what?"

"I stopped at a drug store on my way here this morning." He started to walk back down the hall.

"I hope you got the value pack," she said and saw his grin get bigger.

For one second he thought they might be mis-communicating, but now he knew they were on the same page.

When he rounded the corner into the lunchroom, he saw Jonah sitting at a table. The kid sat up straighter in his chair when Hejazi approached.

"Hey, kid. Are you ready for a rematch?" He sat down and smiled.

"Yeah." Jonah nodded but didn't smile.

"Since you won the last game yesterday, I think you start."

The boy made the first move and they played for a half hour without saying anything. Hejazi won a game and they started to set up the board for the next one when Jonah looked up at him.

"Mr. Hejazi, are you a mercenary?"

"No, I'm not."

"Where are you from?"

"I was born in Chicago."

"That's in the United States, right?"

"Right."

Jonah went quiet again and they continued to play. Hejazi knew the youngster thought hard about something other than the game.

Grace brought them a plate of fresh fried apple fritters floating in butter and dusted with powdered sugar and they gobbled them down in no time, both licking the butter off their fingers.

Before the next game started, Jonah moved to the chair next to Hejazi.

"Sir, yesterday you said you weren't a cop, but that you did security."

"That's right." Hejazi sat back in his chair and watched the boy.

"Can I hire you?"

"Do you need protection?"

"No, everybody here is nice. I want you to save my brother, Jacob. I don't have any money, but I can sweep really good. If you have a garage or driveway, I could work it off."

Hejazi leaned forward. "Let's hold off on the sweeping for a minute. Why do you think your brother needs to be saved?"

The puppy eyes looked up at him. "When we were still together, Feathertop took Jacob away one night. When Jake came back his eye was black and he had bruises all over him. That's when he brought me here to the Haven and told me to wait for him."

"Jonah, did your brother say what happened to him?"

"He just said that Feathertop and a couple of the other men were mean to him." The kid's eyes filled with tears.

Hejazi felt his heart break, but he also became angry. "Jonah, what do you remember about the place where you stayed?"

"It was by water. I heard a loud horn all the time and Jacob said it was a big boat."

"Was it a house or apartment?"

"No, it was a big building. It had a couple of floors and there were parts we weren't allowed to go."

Hejazi nodded. "Were the men ever mean to you?"

"No, Jacob wouldn't let them and he got me out."

"Got you out? What do you mean?"

"We couldn't just leave whenever we wanted. We had to have permission. Jacob snuck me out in the middle of the night." The boy put his hand on Hejazi's arm. "Please, can you help? I'm really scared for Jacob."

He put his big hand over Jonah's. "Let me see what I can find out. I need your permission to bring in some of my men to help me."

"Are they nice?"

"Yes, they are."

"Then okay. That will be all right, but I can only sweep for you."

"Don't worry about the sweeping. Is it okay with you if I tell Miss McKay and Mrs. Black?"

"Not Mrs. Black, she would get scared and it might hurt the baby."

"Good thinking." He looked at his watch. "Why don't we get something other than fritters for lunch and then I'll get to work for you."

They ate a little lunch, and he waited for Grace to finish in the kitchen. He saw her dry her hands before he joined her at the sink.

"Grace, is there a computer I can use around here?"

"Yeah, come with me."

Hejazi spent some time looking at images of the Stockton waterfront and San Joaquin River. He found a couple of locations that could be the building. Pulling his cell phone out of his pocket he called a few of his men and asked them if they'd like to earn some extra cash. All four said yes, but they couldn't get to Stockton until the next day.

Grace came in and brought him a cup of coffee.

"Thanks," he said and took a sip.

Leaning against the desk, she looked down at him and wound her fingers with his. "What have you found?"

"Jonah wants to hire me to find his brother and mentioned that at the place where they were held he heard a boat horn. I've found a couple of places down at the waterfront that are possibilities." He looked up at her. "I've called some of my men to come help, but they won't be here until tomorrow. Want to go for a ride?"

She smiled and nodded. "You bet. I'll go get my bag and let Rae know what we're up to. I don't want her to worry."

"Jonah doesn't want to scare her, so keep it low key, okay?" He opened her hand, kissed the palm and bit her thumb.

"Aye, aye, Sarge." She laughed.

"Captain."

"What?"

"I was a captain."

"Damn, you out rank me." She looked up at the ceiling and tapped her chin. "I can live with it though."

Chapter Five

They drove up and down the waterfront several times and finally saw a big burley bald man with broad shoulders walking with four boys. The kids looked to be in their teens and wore dour looks on their faces.

Hejazi slowly followed them and Grace acted as though she looked for a specific address. They watched as the boys went down a walkway by an old, rundown building and went through a side door.

He turned the Bronco around and they found a parking spot in a lot across the street from the building. It was an old, two-story, wooden structure that jutted out over the water on concrete pilings.

As they watched, kids and a couple of adults came and went. Hejazi took pictures with his cell phone. They needed to get a picture of Jacob so they'd know what he looked like. He hoped Jonah could identify some of the other players, too.

Things slowed down a bit and Hejazi stretched his arms out. His knuckles touched Grace's cheek. He noticed she held her purse tight on her lap and it made him wonder.

"Are you carrying?"

She looked at him. "I do have a license."

"What is it?"

"A baby Glock. It's a little bigger than the originals, but not the 17 size. What about you?"

"I have a Smith and Wesson in a holster on my seat." He saw her nod.

"Nine millimeter?"

"Yeah." He got warm. "Grace, you are so incredibly sexy at this moment. I think I've died and gone to heaven."

She laughed. "All because I said nine millimeter?"

"And Glock." Hejazi squirmed in his seat. "Shit, I've lost my focus. Let's head back. I want Jonah to look at the pictures and see if he can identify anyone. When we finish with him, how about we head over to your place, get a bag packed, and then go back to my hotel for a night of debauched love making?"

Grace laughed. "Debauched, huh? I like the sound of that, but my apartment would be free of charge for you."

"That's true, but the hotel is closer to Haven. After we get this straightened out with the brother and all, then I'll be happy to stay with you."

"Jarrah, how old are you?"

"Thirty-nine, but this is making me feel like a teenager."

"I like both the older and younger versions,

they're both kick ass."

They arrived at Safe Haven just as the kids sat down to dinner. Grace set up the computer, found a fire-wire so he could hook up his cell phone, and then went off to get them some food.

Hejazi went through the photos and put them into a folder. Then he contacted his office to get them started on identifying who they could. It would be tough with the kids, but the adults might have criminal histories that they might track.

Grace brought him a plate of bratwurst and baked beans piled high. In her other hand was a large bowl of salad.

"I don't think I can eat all this," he said as she pulled up a chair.

"You won't have to. We're sharing. I only have two hands and didn't want to make fifteen trips back and forth to the kitchen." She reached into her back pocket and produced two sets of silverware wrapped in paper napkins.

He chuckled. "I love your organization, Grace. I may have to steal you away from the Haven. Can I call you Gracie?"

She looked at him and scooped up some baked beans. "My mom and dad call me Gracie, so I suppose it's okay. Can I call you Jar Jar?" He almost spit up the beans.

"Hmm...I'm not a *Star Wars* character, but when

we're alone if you want to call me Binky, I wouldn't mind." He cut the bratwurst and fed her a piece.

"Does Jarrah mean something?" she asked.

"In the native Arabic Hejaz tongue it means *vessel*. It is said that people with this name have a strong desire for love and companionship. I'm working on that." He placed a piece of brat in his mouth. "Sweetheart, when was the last time you dated?"

"I was engaged to another officer in the Marines. The plan was that we'd get out together and get married. However, he decided he didn't want to leave the service, and re-upped for another six years without telling me." She shrugged. "We decided we weren't on the same page and broke it off. It happened before I came home to Salem a year ago."

They shared the food and continued to feed one another. He looked at Grace and saw she was still serious.

"Jarrah, do you think we can find Jonah's brother?"

"I don't know, but I hope so. Jonah is a good kid and if the authorities ever find his mother, I'd like to give her a piece of my mind."

"That's the hard part, isn't it? The way parents could care less or have too many problems of their own to watch out for their kids. It kills me. Have you read our mission statement?"

"Yeah, I glanced at it."

"We don't rat the kids out to the authorities. If

they ask us to help find family, then we do, but they're pretty anonymous here. In fact, there's a state representative on Rae's back who wants to pass a law that says we have to inform child services of every kid who comes through the door. If we did that we'd lose those kids' trust."

Grace started to get up from the desk and he reached for her hand. "You have a good heart, Miss McKay." He pulled her toward him and gave her a quick kiss.

"I'll take the plates out and track down Jonah," she said and smiled. "Get the photos ready, Captain."

Hejazi chuckled and checked off the steps he needed to take with this. He wanted to be careful with Jonah, but if he hadn't gotten a picture of Jacob then he didn't want the kid to be disappointed. Hejazi felt determined to find the brother and break up that pick-pocket ring.

He heard a knock on the door and saw Jonah peek in. "Hi, Mr. Hejazi. Miss Grace said you needed to show me something."

"Yes, I do, come on in and pull up a chair." He looked for a piece of paper and took a couple of blank sheets out of the printer. He then stood up. "Why don't you sit in this chair?" After the kid sat, Hejazi leaned on the desk with the paper by his leg. "I've got some pictures for you to look through. If you see anyone you know tell me, okay?"

"Sure."

Hejazi leaned over and moved the mouse over the folder. The first picture came up.

"Hey, you found the building. How'd you find it so fast?"

"Jonah, you gave me solid clues to work from. I couldn't have done it without what you told me."

"Cool." The kid smiled for the first time and Hejazi ruffled his hair.

He showed Jonah how to use the mouse and they started through the pictures. If the kid identified anyone in the shots, Hejazi made a note.

"That's Feathertop," Jonah said and pointed at the screen.

Hejazi saw an older, scrawny man with a long beard and long thinning blondish-gray hair. "Jonah, did you ever hear him called by any other name?"

"Not that I remember. Another man, Tyler, just called him *boss*."

They went through a couple more pictures. Jonah sat up straight in the chair and put his hand on the screen. Hejazi saw a look of longing in the kids eyes.

"That's him, that's Jacob. God, he looks skinny." He folded his hands in his lap and looked up at Hejazi with those sad brown eyes. "I miss him. He's all I got."

Hejazi looked at the kid in the shot and saw Jonah's hair color and eyes. He looked like he could be way older than fourteen.

"Can I have a copy of the picture, Mr. Hejazi?"

"I don't see why not." He turned on the printer

next to the computer and got a black and white picture printed. There were two more shots with Jacob that he printed, too.

"Sir, there's one guy you need to watch out for, he's really mean. His name is Gabriel." Jonah held the pictures of Jacob to his chest.

"Did you see him in the pictures?"

"No."

"Did he do something to you?"

"No, but everyone was scared of him, even the older men. One night, during dinner and some of the girls were bringing us food, Gabriel said girls were only meant to be slaves and they were in training for their new jobs. He slapped them a lot." He looked down at his hands. "One time Feathertop told some of us about the guy called the Pied Piper. He said Gabriel was like the Piper when he'd collect the dirty rats and lead them away."

"Now, see, Jonah. That's another clue. I'm sure it will help us out. If you think of anything else, tell me or Grace, okay?"

The kid nodded and they finished with the pictures. Jonah turned to him.

"What's the plan now?"

"I'm going to send the information you gave me to some people I know and see what they can find out. Four of my men will be here in the morning and we'll get a plan laid down to get your brother out of there."

Jonah stood, moved up to him and wrapped his

arms around Hejazi's neck. "Thank you, sir. I need him back."

He held Jonah tight. "You're welcome. Everything is going to work out. I promise."

"Hi, Miss McKay."

"Hey Jonah."

He heard Grace's voice and loosened his hold to look over his shoulder. She smiled at him and he winked back at her.

"Did you guys identify some of the people in the pictures?" She came into the office and stood next to Hejazi.

"Jonah did ID a lot of them. We're sitting pretty."

"And Mr. Hejazi printed the ones of Jacob for me." Jonah showed her the pages.

"Wow, you look alike, only he looks older," she said.

"Well, duh. He *is* my brother," Jonah huffed and looked annoyed.

"Duh?" She tickled the boy. "Okay, Charlie is putting together sundae's over in the cafeteria. Did you eat dinner?"

"Yes, ma'am."

"You head over and save us a seat. We'll be there in a couple of minutes." She turned him to the door.

Hejazi watched him leave and then turned to her. "Five for five," he said.

"What does that mean in Hejazi lingo?" She leaned against him.

"It means that in every single photo Jonah identified someone and he said something that I want to understand better."

"What?"

"He had a hard time telling me who some of the girls were. When I asked him about it, he said the girls don't stay very long and they're kept separate from the boys."

"Jarrah, you're not thinking..."

"I'm not sure what to think. We won't know anything until we get in there. Hopefully, since Jacob's been there for a while he'll be able to tell us more and we can get that place closed down."

"Do you think Jacob will be receptive to talking?"

"We'll have to wait and see." He put his hands on her hips and tilted his head to look at her. "You have a concerned look on your face, babe. There's nothing we can do yet."

"I know, but I'm not sure I want to know why the girls disappear. It can't be good."

He disconnected his phone from the computer and saw he had two messages. After he read the texts he smiled at Grace.

"Two of my men are already here. I'll meet with them in the morning."

"We'll meet with them in the morning," she said.

"Grace..."

"You are not leaving me out of this, Jarrah. Remember, I carry a Glock."

"Man, I love it when you say that word. The way it rolls off your tongue gives me goose bumps." He felt torn and didn't know if she could handle herself in this type of situation but wanted to trust her. "We'll meet them together. They're going to have to meet you anyway. I want them to know you."

She stepped up to him and gave him a light kiss. "Let's go get a sundae. We can discuss this later," she said. "Tonight in bed, I'm pretty sure I won't have any problem convincing you of my abilities. I'll have to get the cuffs out of my bag."

Hejazi wasn't certain he'd heard her right. "Babe are you into bondage?" he whispered.

She grinned. "Maybe I am." Her lips brushed against his, but he pulled his head back. "You'll just have to wait and see."

"I've never...I mean, never..."

"After we get all of this straightened out, we'll have a lot to learn about each other. We'll have a long discussion about what we want."

"That sounds very adult." He put his mouth over hers and felt her tongue run along his lips. Their tongues danced together and he felt flames light up in the lower half of his body.

"Jarrah, how about we say goodnight and skip the sundaes. I'm feeling very horny and I'm off work now anyway."

"Get your bag. I'll meet you in the cafeteria."

Chapter Six

He started the engine and backed out of the parking space. "Sweetheart, there's a brown paper bag behind the seat. Can you grab it?" He heard the bag rustle.

"Jez, you did get the value pack."

"Grace, I'm heading straight for my hotel which is closer than your apartment. If you want to hold off, speak now, because I want you so badly I'm hurting."

"Jarrah, as long as we get there safely, without running red lights or getting pulled over, I have no complaints."

He grinned. "I think I should warn you that you're not getting rid of me."

She smiled back. "Who said anything about getting rid of you? I want you around for a while, bud."

When they got to his room at the Holiday Inn, Hejazi opened the door and let her go in first. She kicked off her shoes and slipped her top over her head. She put her hands around her back to unlatch her bra.

"Wait," he said, walking up to her. He cupped one breast and moved his thumb over her nipple through the lace. "Beautiful." He looked into her sultry eyes and

49

placed his lips on hers.

Grace's hands pulled his shirt out of his pants and when all of the buttons were undone she slowly pushed it off his shoulders and let it drop to the floor.

"I knew you had a nice chest." She kissed around his pecs and undid the button on his pants.

He reached behind her to unhook the bra and let it slide down her arms. "Babe, lie down on the bed," he whispered.

With his pants undone, he moved over her and sucked her lips, and then moved down to kiss and play with her breasts.

"Grace, you are so beautiful."

"Jarrah, you are, too. I love your pants and briefs, and hope you'll take those off soon so I can get a better look."

He propped up on his elbow looking down into her eyes. "We have the whole night to play."

****

She knew if she told any one of her friends that she'd screwed a man she'd only known for two days, they'd think she had loose morals. It didn't matter, he'd caught her hook-line-and-sinker. She'd been attracted to him since he first appeared at the Safe Haven, and the fact that he felt the same way made this *all* right.

Grace lay in his arms and felt wonderful. "Jarrah?"

"Yeah."

"Where do you live?" She moved her arm and

propped her head in her hand so she could look at him.

"I have a condo in El Segundo. It's about twenty miles from L.A. I haven't been there for about six weeks."

"El Segundo is along the coast, right?"

"Yep, not far from L.A. International Airport. It's a small community with nice people. I also like being near beach."

She knew she'd gotten way ahead of herself. This was only the first time they'd been together, but she wanted to ask him how long he planned to stay, could she visit him in his home, and such. *You need to just relax, sister.*

Hejazi put his arm behind his head. "You know what? I think I may have some changes coming."

"Like what?"

"I think this might be a good time to make some adjustments. For the last year I've wanted to turn over the field work to one of my senior men. I'd still run the company but wouldn't be out in the field so much."

She put her hand flat on his chest. "Have you lost interest in guarding people?"

"No, no. It's just..." he sat up and leaned against the headboard. "I'm going to be forty this year and I've been thinking I need something...no, strike that, not something, I need someone to share life with. I've cut myself off from relationships for way too long."

She sat up next to him. Seeing some concern in his eyes, she wanted to make this an easy conversation.

"What's on your mind?"

"Babe, I think we have something we need to continue exploring. I never believed I'd ever feel like this, but I do," he said.

"I didn't believe it possible before yesterday, but I'm beginning to wonder." Her hands moved up to his neck. "Jarrah, this may sound nuts, but there's something between us...I don't know, its karma or kismet or good juju. I feel it strongly for you."

He kissed her long and gentle. When his head moved back she saw moisture in his eyes. "I feel it, too," he whispered. "Last night, I asked myself what the point of being alone solved over the years. I didn't like the answer."

"What was the answer?"

"Nothing. I couldn't come up with a single thing that it solved. It jolted me awake and if you'd asked me to wait for you for months, I would have waited."

She put her hand on his cheek. "Jarrah, I believe you."

Chapter Seven

Hejazi parked his Bronco in the same spot across from the waterfront building he'd been in yesterday. His four men and Grace were positioned and ready to go. They'd all been ready for the last two hours. There'd been no movement.

Last night, after loving on each other, he wrapped his arms around Grace and held her tightly, thanking God for sending her. He didn't want to give her up. He remembered the conversation.

He'd rolled onto his side and propped up on his elbow. "Grace, we need to talk about tomorrow."

"Okay."

"When I'm in work mode, I tend to focus down one-hundred percent. If I treat you like one of the guys or act a little distant, I don't want you to think it's you. I'm too much of a perfectionist."

"I get it and it makes sense. Turner Black said the way your team worked amazed him when you saved Rae. Treat me like one of the team, no holds barred. I thought of something, too." She adjusted and looked at him. "I don't think I should be in the detail that brings in Jacob. He may have seen me at Haven and it could scare him off."

"That's good thinking. I'll team you up with

Griggsy. He's our helicopter pilot and can find shadows in a pitch black room. He's also a climber and the guys tease him about being a monkey."

He watched the building across from him and felt glad he'd teamed her with Griggs. They moved into a dark doorway next to the warehouse and he was impressed with Grace's skills. She kept up with Monkey-boy well.

Hejazi looked through his binoculars and saw nothing move.

When Griggs, Jones, Rand and Jack arrived in his hotel room at four o'clock in the morning, they'd accepted Grace on the spot. All she'd said was she'd been in the Marines. The snarky remarks started after they polished off two pots of coffee. Hejazi thought he should have warned her about the teasing, but she seemed aware of this behavior.

"I suppose your screwing the Chief?" Jonesy said *and tipped his straight-back chair on two legs.*

"What if I am?" Grace finished loading her *Glock.*

"It's about time. We were beginning to think he might not like women." He grinned.

"No, that's you, asshat." Rand, his partner, hit him in the shoulder hard.

The other men laughed and Grace smiled.

"I don't know, Gracie, his dick is pretty old. You sure you don't want some younger meat?" Jonesy continued to tease.

"If you mean yours, Jonesy,"—she snickered and rolled her eyes—*"I think I'd rather have a mature man. A mature dick has staying power."* She stared him down and arched an eyebrow.

Jonesy laughed and he high-fived her. "Wow, you know how to hit below the belt. Me like. You're going to fit in just fine, sweetheart."

"Besides, Jonesy, you're what? Three years younger than the chief?" Rand said.

Hejazi laughed at the memory. As much shit as those men dished, she'd given right back. There were a couple of times that he'd almost called out-of-bounds, but she'd cut them down a size.

"Hey, Chief?" he heard Rand.

"Yep."

"We've got movement. There are three adults, five kids coming out the east side and moving down the sidewalk."

"Can you ID our target?"

"Yeah, the kid from the pictures is with them."

"Okay, Jonesy, Rand follow behind them. Jack stay here and watch the warehouse. Griggs and Grace, get in the second Bronco after they leave the area. Grace, you know the neighborhood, any ideas where they might be headed?"

"No, Cap. There's not a lot down here."

"Chief, they've stopped at a bus stop. Want us to follow?"

"Affirmative. How far down the road are you?"

"About seven blocks."

"Okay, Griggsy, let's head down and park a block away." Hejazi started his vehicle.

"Chief, we're almost on them. Going silent."

They waited for about ten minutes a block from the transit stop and Hejazi saw a bus in his review mirror. He announced it to the men and they waited another couple of minutes.

"This is Rand. We're on the bus."

"Here we go, Griggs. Let's follow them." He moved onto the road.

"Cap, I think they're headed for Weberstown Mall," he heard Grace.

"Roger that."

They continued to follow and when the bus pulled into a huge transfer center, Hejazi turned into the parking lot for the mall. The bus unloaded and five kids and three adults stepped off and started across the lot. When he saw Rand and Jones start to follow, he knew he needed to switch them up.

"Jonesy, Rand split up. Work a trade-off."

"Roger, Chief."

"Griggs, you take over the tail of our target when they get inside. Grace and I will bring up the rear."

He got out of the SUV and teamed with Grace, while Griggs moved to catch up with Rand and Jones.

As they walked toward the mall, Grace looked at him. "If they can stay with Jacob, he won't be able to hide anywhere."

"What do you mean *if?* Sweetheart, we can follow a needle through a haystack," he heard one of the men say.

Hejazi smiled at her. "Earbuds. Everyone hears everything."

"What was that, sir," Rand asked.

"Nothing. Were entering the north end. Where are we?"

"The kids split off, targets on his own with one adult. They're just passing The Footlocker and headed south," Griggs said.

"I'm pulling ahead of them, Chief."

"Okay Rand stay in front. Griggsy continue behind. Jonesy where are you?"

"Almost even on the opposite side."

"Chief, it looks like they're going into pick mode."

Hejazi knew they followed and watched the kid as he picked from purses and bags. If it was like at the Veronda concert, the kid would swing back around and hand off the wallet to the adult handler.

"Chief, they're going into Penney's. What do you think?" Rand asked.

"We need to cut him off from the handler. Grace and I can deal with it."

"Are you going to tag him?"

"No, we're going to do a reverse-damsel-in-distress. You guys close in on target." Hejazi turned to Grace. He took out his earbud and motioned for her to do the same. "Okay, babe, a quick lesson in the reverse-damsel. We get behind the handler. You'll be in the middle with me slightly behind."

"And you're going to knock me into him, grab my purse and I distract him," she said

Hejazi grinned. "God damn, I think I love you."

"Speaking of, you're making me want you, a lot."

"Yeah, well, I won't mention my own thoughts. Keep it straight for a little bit longer and then we'll get some pressure relieved."

"It's a date." She smiled and put her earbud back in. "Ready, Cap?"

"Here we go. We meet back at the Bronco."

Hejazi watched Grace walk into Penney's, counted to ten and then followed her. The handler stood by a display in the middle of the store. Their target weaved between the racks and obviously looked for someone to pick.

Grace strolled up alongside the handler and looked at the display case.

"We got him, Chief."

Hejazi moved toward Grace and bumped her into the handler. He grabbed her bag and ran to the exit.

When he was one-hundred feet away from the entrance, he turned into a shoe store and stood by a window. Concern for Grace's safety crashed into his gut and he started to sweat.

****

Grace landed on top of the handler who splayed

out on his back. She looked down at the guy and tried to act scared.

"Shit, I'm sorry, but that man stole my purse. God, where's security? Are you okay?" She started to push herself up and the man stood with her.

"Security? Lady, the guy ran out of the store." He pointed at the entrance.

Grace saw a cashier. "Ma'am someone just stole my purse. This guy saw him. Can you call security, please?"

"No. I didn't see the guy at all. He ran out of the store. Penney's security won't do anything," the handler said and started to walk away.

She bit her cheek to keep from laughing. Of course, the guy wouldn't want security around. She'd felt a bunch of wallets stuffed inside the handlers jacket.

"Can you call the mall cops then?"

"Miss, you'll have to go out to the information desk and have them called from there. We can't call them," the cashier said.

"Great, just fucking great. The guy will be all the way to Sacramento by the time I get any help." She huffed as she walked away from the handler and headed back into the mall.

Walking back the way they'd come in, she acted like she looked for the information desk. She felt a warm hand wrap around her elbow and they kept moving.

"We're clear. Where are you?" Hejazi said and handed her the purse.

"The kids giving us an earful, Chief. We're back at the Bronco's," she heard.

"Get him back to Haven. We're right behind you."

Chapter Eight

When Hejazi and Grace got back to the Bronco, they saw the other team was gone. He trusted his men with his life and didn't see any reason to reconnect with them.

The drive back to Safe Haven was quiet. For some reason he felt a little uncomfortable with Grace and couldn't think of a reason why.

When they pulled into a parking space in front of Haven, he shut the car off and stayed in his seat.

"Jarrah, do you think we're moving too fast?" Grace asked. "We only met three days ago."

He stared out the front window. "Why do you think that?"

"For one thing you won't look at me and you've pulled away from me. It wasn't because of *work mode*, either."

"No. When I left you in Penney's with that handler..."

He turned his head only to see a concerned look on her beautiful face. Her eyebrows were creased and she wore a deep frown. He tried to focus on why he felt out of sorts and it hit him like a bolt of lightning.

"No, we're fine." He shook his head and reached for her hand. "I've worked a lot of tough cases and even tougher clients. I've always prided myself on my focus. This is the first time I've ever gone off the grid. After I left you in the store I worried about your safety. I started to sweat. It's not you or us, babe." He kissed her hand.

"That's a relief. I thought maybe I'd scared you off."

"Not a chance."

Grace laughed. "Thank you for worrying about me, but remember one thing, sweetie. You are a human and allowed to hiccup once in a while."

"Who me? Never. I want you to participate with my detail. You're very good under pressure." He leaned over and gave her a kiss. "And you don't scare me, yet."

She smiled. "Hmm...I'll have to work on that."

He kissed her again and then sat up. "We better get inside. I want to talk with Jacob."

They walked side by side up the front steps into the main lobby. The big man behind the desk looked at them.

"They're up in Rae's office," he said.

When they reached the top floor, they saw Hejazi's team standing in the hallway with Rae.

"Where's Jacob?" Hejazi asked.

Rae pointed at the door. "Jonah's in there talking to him."

"How long?"

"About twenty minutes," Rand said.

"Chief, you may want to re-plug in. Jack's reporting from the warehouse." Griggs held his hand cupped to his ear.

Hejazi took the earbuds from his pocket and handed one to Grace.

"...returned. The one identified as Feathertop just drove up and he looks pissed," Jack said.

"Jack, I missed the first part. Would you repeat?" Hejazi looked at Grace.

"The group you followed earlier is back minus one. Rand said they got the kid. Chief, do you want me to keep watching the warehouse?"

"Affirmative. These guys will relieve you in an hour." He looked at his watch. "I'll let you guys decide the schedule. I want eyes on that place twenty-four/seven."

"I'll team up with Jack now and you guys relieve us," Griggs said and started down the hall.

He turned to Grace. "I'm going to talk to the kid. Why don't you come in with me? I need a mother figure."

He knocked on the door and walked into the office with Grace behind him.

"Mr. Hejazi!" He heard Jonah's voice and then the kid wrapped his arms around Hejazi's waist. "Thank you so much for saving my brother."

"Shut the fuck up, Jonah. He didn't save

anything." Jacob paced by the windows.

Jonah stepped back and looked up at Hejazi. "Jake's being a jerkwad."

"It's okay, I've dealt with worse. Listen kid, I need to talk with Jacob for a couple of minutes. Can you wait outside with Mrs. Black?"

"Sure." The kid looked back at his brother. "Jake, Mr. Hejazi is one of the good guys," he said and walked out.

Jacob's hair was light brown and he had the same eyes as his brother. He stood by the window with his arms crossed and wore a deep scowl.

"Why don't we sit down and talk," Hejazi said.

"Fuck you," the teenager said and turned to look out the window.

Hejazi walked over to him, grabbed the back of his jacket and steered him to a chair. "I said let's sit and talk."

The boy wouldn't look at him and Hejazi went silent. He watched the kids face for signs. After ten minutes the kid's eyes turned to stare back at him.

"I thought you wanted to talk," Jacob said.

"I do."

The kid held out his hands. "What?"

"What's your favorite sport?"

Jacob frowned. He shook his head. "Wrestling."

"WWF or ECW?"

"WAKO."

"That's not wrestling." Hejazi leaned forward.

"I just wanted to see if you were still awake, old man."

"You like kickboxing?"

"How long are you going to keep me here?" Jacob sat back in the chair.

"Are you hungry?" He wouldn't answer the kid's questions yet.

"I need to go back to the warehouse."

"Why?"

"That's none of your fucking business."

Hejazi watched the kids face and it became a kaleidoscope of emotions. What he saw the most was hurt and innocence lost. He'd seen the same thing in Jonah's eyes.

He continued to stare at Jacob and after a minute the kid broke the stare. "I have to go back, because my girlfriend is still there. I have to protect her."

"From what?"

Jacob went silent and looked back at him.

"Do you need to protect her from Feathertop or one of his men? Are they abusing the girls?"

Jacobs jaw clenched and after a couple of minutes, the kids eyes welled and a tear rolled down his cheek.

"Jacob, are they abusing the girls?" Hejazi softened his tone.

The kid swallowed and nodded. "After they're spoiled, Feathertop sells them. They're shipped overseas or go down south."

Hejazi straightened in his chair and looked over his shoulder at Grace. "Babe, would you go out for a minute?"

"Yep." She left the office.

He knew, she and his men all wore their earbuds and would be able to hear the conversation. When the door shut he looked back at Jacob.

"Kid, did any of the adults abuse you?"

The teenager jerked in his chair as if he'd been hit and Hejazi knew the answer.

"Did the old man touch you?"

Jacob leaned over and put his head in his hands. "That motherfucker..." he hissed.

"Jonah told me about someone called Gabriel. Did he treat you bad?"

The kid stared at him. "He's Feathertop's kid and..." He started to choke up and another tear dripped off his cheek.

"I get the picture. Are the other boys abused, too?"

Jacob stared at him. "Some of them like it. Some of the older boys...fuck, they'll do it to any of the younger boys or girls. My girlfriend hasn't been used yet, but they're going to spoil them tonight. That's what the adults call it. Spoiling. They just get fucked and then sold." Jacob turned away from him and Hejazi knew he struggled.

"Okay, look at me." He watched the brown eyes turn to him. "You don't know me for shit, right? I swear to you, the people here at Haven are trustworthy. They're here to help not hurt. Will you give me twenty-four hours?"

"To do what?"

"To get your girl out of there."

"You don't have twenty-four hours, mister."

"I know."

"Do you think you can get her out?" Jacob whispered.

"I'll need to go over this with my team before I can give you an answer."

The kid held out his right hand. "Swear it."

Hejazi grabbed his hand. "You, too."

They shook and then Hejazi sat back. "I need some information."

"Like what?"

"I need to know everything you can tell me about the warehouse. Where the kids are held and where the men hang out. If you could draw pictures of the layout, that would be great. Will you do that for me?"

Jacob stared at him and after a few seconds he nodded. "There's no electronic security in the building."

Hejazi stood, went to the door and opened it. He looked into the hallway and saw Grace. "Babe, I need two legal pads and some pens."

"And a ruler," Jacob said behind him.

"And a ruler." He smiled at her.

"Mister, before I forget. They keep the girls in

cages on the top floor," Jacob said.

Hejazi looked up at the door hinge and found a way to prop it open. "We need some air in here. Jacob, do you want anything to eat or drink?"

"Do they have Pepsi in this place?"

"We'll find out."

Grace came in and put the legal pads and pens on the desk.

"Babe, Jacob would like a Pepsi and I could use a cup of coffee. I know you're not a waitress, but would you mind?"

"No, I don't mind. I might even scrounge up a couple of sandwiches and chips."

"Great, thank you." He turned and saw Jacob already working on a pad of paper.

Chapter Nine

Grace watched them work and talk. Hejazi filled up many pages on the legal pad. The kid drew several versions of the warehouse looking at it from different angles. Impressed with his ability, she asked him if he'd thought of going to school for architecture. When the kid said maybe, but he wanted to draw comic books, she'd almost started to cry and became more determined than ever to help him reach his dream.

After three and half hours, Hejazi decided he needed a break. He called his men and told them to come back. Jonah showed his brother around Haven and filled him in on the rules.

After the kids left the office, Grace walked up behind Hejazi and started to massage his neck and shoulders.

"Ah, sweetheart, that feels good." He leaned his head back against her stomach and looked up at her.

"You've been working hard, Captain."

"The guys will be back shortly and we'll have a roundtable to determine how to handle this, if we handle it."

Grace stopped and moved to his side so she could see his eyes. "What do you mean *if?*"

"I've been in touch with the FBI. If they say no to my proposal, we're dead in the water." His fingers moved to lace with hers. "Don't be disappointed yet, Grace."

"I'm not so much disappointed as I am pissed. We have to get those kids out of there. After what Jacob said..."

"I know, we will get them, I promise. I'm hoping it will be sooner than later, because if that old man suspects anything, we will be finished. I want us to do it, too. If the Feds get their hands on those kids, they'll wind up in the system and God only knows where they'll end up."

"Maybe we should keep the FBI out of the loop and just take the kids ourselves. We can help them out from here, better than the system can."

"Babe, we have to stay within the law. We can skirt some issues, but for the most part we have to do the right thing legally for the kids. Okay?"

"I suppose. I don't have to like it."

There was a tap on the door and they both looked up.

"Knock, knock. Hi, Chief."

Two men of equal height walked into the office and set duffle bags on the floor. "We were in the neighborhood and thought we'd stop by."

"Taylor, Jerry what are you doing here? You're supposed to be with your families."

"Jack called and said you needed help. Here we

are," the dark haired man said.

"It's okay, Chief. Monica understands," the blond added.

"Grace, this is Taylor and Jerry. Two more of my team."

She shook her head. "I'd better make some more coffee."

****

The other four men came back to Haven and they all proceeded to discuss possible scenarios for getting the kids out of the warehouse. Several plans were laid on the table and they threw around plus and minus options.

"Chief, this looks like there's a couple of skylights on the roof. I could go through there," Griggs said and showed them one of Jacob's drawings.

There was a knock on the door and two navy blue suited men walked in.

"Henry, glad you could make it." Hejazi stood up and shook hands with the tall, thin man.

"We would have been here sooner, but the computer was backed up." The agent threw a folder onto the table and loosened his tie. "I'm Henry Tanado, for those I haven't met and this is my partner, Bob Sims. The picture of the old guy you sent came up aces. His name is Frank Magnus and we've been watching him for years. We've never been able to peg him with anything though. Our legal department is working on a search warrant to check the warehouse."

"How long will that take?" Jack asked.

"It could take up to a week, but I'm hoping that when the kids are mentioned it will be signed off sooner," Agent Tanado said.

Hejazi sat back and felt his shoulders tense up again. "We don't have that long."

"Jarrah?" a woman's voice said from the door.

He looked and saw Rae. "Do you need your office back?"

"No. I just got a call from the front desk downstairs. There are two men here and they're looking for Jacob."

Hejazi stood up and thought for a second. "Jack, Griggsy come with me. The rest of you, ear buds in and move down to the second floor landing and hold position." He started to leave the room and Agent Tanado grabbed his arm.

"We'll come down with you, Hejazi," the agent said.

When he walked into the hallway he saw Rae. "Mrs. Black, please stay up here. Turner wouldn't want you to get involved with this."

"Just be careful, okay?" Rae said. "I'll be on the second floor with the team."

Hejazi didn't want her anywhere near this situation, but it was her establishment. Starting toward the stairs, he put his earbud in and snapped the leather off his gun in the holster under his arm.

When he got down to the first floor, he saw the

old man and the handler from this morning at the mall.

Griggs and Jack stood at his sides and they stopped at the bottom of the stairs and stared at the old man.

"And who might you be?" Feathertop asked as his employee leaned over and spoke in his ear.

"I guess your man just told you who I am." Hejazi crossed his arms and waited.

"I think you have one of my boys here. We call him Hawk, but his real name is Jacob Sullivan. I'd like to speak with him."

"Grace, would you check with Jacob and see if he is willing to speak with Mr. Magnus."

"Roger that," he heard in his ear.

"Who are you speaking to, Mr...?" Feathertop asked.

"Hejazi. I'm speaking to myself."

"I see you want to play games."

"No, I don't play games, I assure you."

"We're coming down, Cap," Grace said.

He continued to stare at the old man and heard footsteps on the stairs. Turning halfway, he saw them start down the last flight and put his hand up to stop her and Jacob.

"That's the bitch that crashed into me and said her purse was stolen, boss," the handler said.

"Better watch it, asshole. She's my woman and I don't take kindly to anyone calling her derogatory names." Hejazi lowered his hands into fists.

"My apologies, Mr. Hejazi. I'll need to speak with my staff about being offensive." Magnus looked up at Jacob. "Hawk, it's time to come home. Those who care for you will be leaving soon."

"Fuck you, Feathertop. If you hurt Heather, I'll kill you. I swear it," Jacob yelled.

Hejazi looked back and saw that Grace held Jacob. He turned and faced the old man. "There you have it. Jacob doesn't wish to speak with you. This is a good time for you to leave the premises."

"Hawk, I'm sorry you feel that way. I hope you do well." The old man turned and started to the exit.

"But boss, we can't let him..." the handler started.

"Shut it, Carter," Feathertop snapped.

Hejazi watched them leave and started back up the stairs. He stopped halfway up and looked in the kids eyes.

"They're going to send the girls away," Jacob said.

"I know." He nodded and looked up at the FBI agents. "Henry, fuck the search warrent. We're moving tonight."

Jacob grabbed Hejazi's shirt. "Sir, will she be okay?"

Chapter Ten

As the sun went down, Hejazi's team changed into black clothes and bullet proof vests, and blackened their faces. They went over final details and waited for a school bus to pull up. It would carry the kids to Safe Haven. The two FBI agents went along with the plan and called in a back up team to join them. They'd arrest the adults who were left in the warehouse. They wanted to nail Magnus to the wall.

"Chief, what do we do if they've cleared out?" Jack asked.

"We find them and take them out. I made a promise to Jacob that we'd bring out his girl."

"Cap, can I shoot Magnus." Grace looked up at him.

"If he threatens, I'll hold him down for you."

"Jesus, Chief. Your girl is fucking hard and I find it really sexy," Rand said.

Hejazi looked at him. "That's the way I like them. It's time to move. Here comes the bus."

They loaded up and started to the warehouse. Rae arranged to have extra help at Haven to get the kids settled and safe. Jacob said there might be fifteen to thirty kids and he wasn't sure how many girls were being held.

They parked two blocks from the target and broke into teams. Hejazi put Grace with Griggs and they hit the fire escape in the back of the building and went up to the roof. There were two large skylights up on top that looked down onto the second floor. They had equipment to remove the glass.

He and Jack would be next to the front door, while the other two teams would go through emergency exits on either side of the warehouse. Jacob said there would be eight to ten adults guarding and Magnus stayed up on the top floor.

"Chief, we're in position," Rand said.

"Team two, in position," Griggs said.

"Copy that, Chief. Taylor and I are good," Jerry said.

There was a light over the front door. Jack took an air-pellet gun out of his pocket, aimed and took out the light. Hejazi locked eyes with him and counted down from three on his fingers. Jack launched at the door and kicked it open. Hejazi followed him in covering the entrance the way they'd been trained in the Marines. There was enough light coming through the windows he could see several cots down the length of the warehouse. Boys sat up and he heard some mumbling. Three tall men started toward them and his other four came through the exits from the back.

"We're on top, Cap," Grace said in his ear.

****

Grace's heart pumped with adrenaline. Griggs

lead the way and helped her make the final part of the climb. She pulled onto the ledge and watched him leap up, grab the edge of the roof and pull himself up. She reached, locked hands with Griggs and he pulled her up.

Monkey was about right, she thought. "We're on top, Cap," she whispered and stood halfway up.

They moved to the skylight and looked through at the second floor. The glass was filthy and splotched with bird poop.

"Shit, literally," Griggs whispered.

He took the glass cutter out of his pocket and while she adjusted suction cups on the window, he started to cut the glass. She made sure the cups wouldn't slip and as he moved around the frame, she latched onto two at one end and held them. He reached for one of the cups, nodded and tapped the glass. It came loose and they lifted it out.

Griggs secured a nylon rope and before he let it down, he leaned through and hanging upside down, took a look. When he came back out, he stopped.

"Huh, Chief, we may have a problem," Griggs said.

Grace looked at him with what she hoped was a question.

"Go Griggsy," Hejazi said.

"The girls are in the cages, but their collared and cuffed. The collars are chained to the cage. It's going to take some time getting them freed."

"Crap, work it Monkey-boy. If you have to hold them there until we clean out the bottom floor, do it," Hejazi ordered.

"Roger that." He looked at Grace. "I'm going down. I'll signal you." And with that he was over the side and down on the floor.

She looked over the side and watched him land on his feet. He put a finger up to his lips and then motioned for her to come down. She hadn't repelled down anything in ages and when she hit the floor, she looked around the room. She held her Glock with both hands and circled around, checking doors that were storage rooms and a bathroom.

When she saw the two cages, there were eight or nine girls staring back at her. They wore baby-doll pajamas. None of them wore shoes and Grace felt appalled by the conditions in which they were being held.

"Which one of you is Heather?" she whispered.

"I am," a small blonde haired, blue eyed cutie said.

"Jacob sent us. You need to hold on. We're going to get you out of there."

Grace heard Griggs make a *psst* noise and looked at him. He pointed at the door and mouthed *Someone's coming.* They both took up positions behind the entrance and she pointed her gun. As the door started to open they moved back to stay behind it. The old man walked in and flipped on a light. Griggs caught him by the arm and jammed his gun into the side of the man's head.

"No movement, old man," Griggs said.

Grace stood behind the door and could see someone else pass the hinge. Griggs stood with his back to the door and she knew he didn't see the other man coming. She took in a deep breath and when the guy appeared, she clocked him on the side of the head with the butt of her gun. Then she brought her knee up hard into his groin. The guy let out a harsh groan and folded onto the floor. She held her gun on him, but the guy didn't move.

"I'm surrounded by amateurs," the old man said.

Griggs sat Feathertop in a chair and used plastic zip ties to attach his wrists to the wooden arms. Then he and Grace cuffed the other guy on the floor.

"Nice move, Gracie. Even my dick hurt with the way your knee caught him." Griggs walked to the cage.

"Thanks, Monkeyboy." She heard a chuckle in her ear bud.

She guarded the two men, while Griggs worked on the cage door locks. They heard shots fired from the ground floor and a lot of chatter started in the earbud.

"Rand, report," she heard Hejazi.

"It's okay, Chief. One of the kids had a gun and he just shot a chair. He's disarmed."

Griggs got the door opened and looked at the collars. "I'm going to cut these off, but we'll have to wait to get the cuffs off," he said to the girls. "I'll need for you to hold real still while I'm cutting. I don't want to slice up your necks."

Grace kept her Glock aimed at the old man. She wanted to kill Feathertop and wished he'd try to get loose.

A fight could be heard in the earbuds and it annoyed her that she didn't know who fought with whom. There were a couple of loud smacks and grunts and then she heard, "Clear on the ground floor."

Griggs cut the collars quickly. "Chief, all the girls are loose. We haven't checked the rest of the second floor," he said.

"Roger that. Team three's on their way up. Hold."

It wasn't Hejazi's voice that she heard and Grace got a knot in her stomach. She didn't realize she'd tensed up until she finally heard his voice.

"The Feds are here. Let's get the kids out ASAP," he said.

Grace's heart rate slowed down.

There was a knock on the door and it started to creek open. "Don't shoot, it's Jerry and Taylor." They came into the room. "Wow, look at what you caught."

"Grace, would you get the girls downstairs." Griggs cut the last collar off.

She turned and stared at Feathertop. "Where are their clothes, asshole?"

He laughed. "We burned them."

"There's a cupboard over here with some blankets," Jerry said. He pulled them out and handed them around to the girls.

Once they were wrapped up, Grace took them down the stairs. Rand met them at the bottom and showed them out to the bus. They got the girls all in and seated. The boys were already in the back.

"Griggsy bring the two assholes down to the ground floor. We'll all meet back at Haven. Rand get that bus moving."

"Roger that."

The door on the bus closed and Grace tucked her Glock into the back of her pants and then sat down for the ride.

When they arrived back at Safe Haven, Grace and Rand got the kids up to the cafeteria. Rae had called in the cooks. They prepared pizza, soup, hot chocolate, and other things. They congregated at two long tables and moved chairs to sit together. Rand worked on the cuffs the girls wore and in about thirty minutes they were freed.

Grace couldn't believe Rae was still on her feet. It was three o'clock in the morning and she looked tired. She told Grace that Jacob helped out in the kitchen. When she looked at the tables, she saw he sat with the girl named Heather.

She got a cup of coffee and sat with a couple of the girls. She explained what would be happening for the next couple of days and said in the morning they'd go to the storeroom on the first floor and find them some clothes and shoes.

"I won't wear no used shit," one of the girls said.

Grace smiled. "The clothes and shoes are all donated and brand new. We have some jackets that are hand-me-downs. They've been cleaned and, if you ask me, some of them are hot."

A couple of the kids laughed and it felt nice to see them smile.

"I suppose you're going to call the cops now," one of the boys said.

"No." Rae walked to the table. "That's not how we run things. We're here to help you, not throw you into the foster-care system. We do expect you to work with us, though. How many of you were taken from your families?"

Grace looked and eight of the ten girls raised their hands.

"If you want to go home to your families, we'll help you get there. The rest of you have other options we'll explain tomorrow. I know right now you have trust issues and I understand, but you're safe here and if you let us, we'll help you the best we can."

The kids started to talk amongst themselves and Rae walked to the kitchen.

"She seems really cool," one of the girls said.

Grace smiled. "She is and one of the best bosses I've ever worked for." She felt a hand on her shoulder and looked up. Hejazi stood over her. "I'll be right back," she said to the table of kids.

"You need to wash your face," she said.

"You, too."

Standing, she took his hand and they walked toward the hallway. They went into the room where they'd kissed the second day they'd known each other.

When the door closed she sucked in her breath. "What happened to your eye and lip?"

"One of the asshole guards thought he'd act tough and tried to beat his way past me." He kissed her and hissed. "No hard kisses for a day or two."

"We need to get you some ice."

"Before that," he wrapped his hands round her waist and pulled her close. "I just want to say how impressed I am with you, Sergeant McKay. Griggsy told me that you kicked ass and I'm so in love with you it hurts even more than my busted lip."

"Yeah? You're in love with me?" She rubbed up against him. "It's a good thing, since I'm loving you, too." She kissed his chin.

"Are you tired?"

"Yep, exhausted. This has been a long day."

"I'm a slave driver. How much longer do you need to stay here?" He pulled her into a tight hug.

"I want to help get the girls settled in and then we can leave."

"Good. Let's do it and then we can get some sleep."

"And ice."

"Right."

A BLAZING DANCE

Chapter Eleven

Hejazi lay on his back and listened to Grace breathe softly. It sounded like music to him and hypnotized him into a hot daydream.

He looked over at her and felt warm. She lay on her side with the bed sheet covering the lower half of her body. Her breasts looked at him between her arms and he moved the back of his hand across her nipple. She started to laugh.

She whispered and opened her eyes, "God, I love waking up with you."

He pushed her onto her back. "I do love you in my bed, woman."

"What time is it?"

"Around ten-thirty." He kissed her breast.

"Jarrah, I have to get to work."

He cupped her breast with his hand and looked up at her. "No, you don't."

"I promised some of those girls we'd get their parents called today."

His eyebrows came together. "What?"

"Eight of the girls were not street kids. They were kidnapped from their homes and I want to help get them back."

He pulled up even with her and put his lips on hers. "I love you so much, Grace. You are a good woman with a big heart. We need to talk about living together or getting married. Let's get a shower and some breakfast and get to work."

He started to move off her, but she stopped him. "Sweetheart, I agree to all that you said. We will discuss it later, but I just wanted you to know now that I agree with you."

He laughed. "I'm going to be walking around with a big-fat-dorky grin on my face all day. Thank God my men are on their way home. I'd never hear the end of it."

"Hey, I'll take them on. I love your dorky grin." She touched his bruised lip. "How's your face feeling?"

"I'll live and I know it makes me ruggedly gorgeous," he laughed. Hejazi got up and walked to her side of the bed. "Come with me, beautiful. I'm going to wash you in the shower. Grinning all day I can handle, but not the thoughts about your body."

She took his hand and he pulled her off the bed.

****

When they arrived back at Safe Haven it was just before noon and the kids were gathering in the cafeteria for lunch. Jonah raced up to Hejazi and thanked him over and over and then the kid dragged him to a table with his brother and some other kids.

Grace smiled and enjoyed the noise in the

lunchroom. Rae walked up beside her and hooked arms.

"This is our biggest crowd yet," Grace said.

"I have two of the boys set up to meet with therapists today. They're the ones Jacob mentioned." Rae arched her eyebrows.

"Yeah, it would be nice to save at least two of them and straighten them out."

"Grace, are you planning to stay with us?"

She looked at Rae and couldn't figure out why she'd ask that. "What are you talking about?"

"Now that you and Hejazi are a couple and you've worked with his team, I thought you might move south to be closer to him."

Grace realized there were a lot of things relationship-wise that she needed to think about.

"We haven't discussed that yet, Rae. We've only know each other a week."

"If you do decide to leave, can I ask you to wait until I get back from maternity leave? I need someone here I can trust."

"Thank you for the compliment, and, yes, I'll definitely... I mean, I love this job and..." She felt anxiety settle in her stomach.

"Grace, I'm sorry. I didn't mean to upset you." Rae squeezed her arm.

"No, I just hadn't thought about it. I will stay until you get back. I promise that."

"Good. I'm going to go see how things are going with the girls. Hopefully, we can get them back to their families."

"That's good." Grace nodded and started to her office.

She sat down behind her desk and put her feet up on the edge. Her knees were against her chest and she put her hands on her head. It gave her a headache trying to decide what she wanted to do, not that she needed to make any decisions today. She thought it would be best to talk with Hejazi, but they'd only been together a short time.

Putting priorities in order in her head, Hejazi and her job were tied for first. This was all she could think about and it started to drive her crazy.

Her head fell on top of the desk with her fingers pulling at her hair. There was a throat cleared and she looked up. Hejazi stood in the doorway.

"Hey, are you okay?"

She leaned forward. "Yeah, close the door."

As the door clicked, he moved around her desk and squatted by her chair. "What's going on?"

She looked down at him and put her hand on his arm. "Rae asked me to run things here at Haven while she's on maternity leave."

"That's great...I mean I think it's great. I know you can handle it." He put his hand on her cheek. "Why? Is there a problem?"

"It's not so much a problem and it is. You know I love working here."

"Right."

"And I've fallen in love with you."

"Yes, and that's a good thing."

"But your home and business are down south and I don't want to lose this job, but if we're so far apart how can we work? Long distance relationships are hard."

"Babe, let's get one thing straight. If you think I'm going away from you, it ain't gonna happen. There's too much I want to do with you. I have a crazy desire to take you camping, to the gun range, and nineteen or twenty thousand other things, but I'm sure there will be more that I want to do. Are we clear?"

She stared at him and nodded.

"I do need to go down to El Segundo to make arrangements to sell my condo. I've spoken to Jack about heading up the staff in L.A. I'm going to become a part-time silent partner. I don't want to be out in the field so much, and if there are any questions, Stockton isn't that far away.

Grace couldn't believe everything he'd just said. "You'd do all that for me? Give up your condo and your business for me?"

"Babe, I'd walk across a flame pit for you. I have a plan coming together in my head and once everything falls into place that will be that." He kissed the back of her hand.

"Really?"

"Yes, really. I see I'll have to convince you tonight." He stood up and leaned over her with his lips above hers. "And, it's a secret," he whispered.

Grace sucked in her breath. "You're keeping secrets from me already?"

Hejazi gave her an evil laugh and kissed her lips. She raked her fingers through his hair and pushed up from the chair. His hand moved around her waist and held her tight.

She pulled back and looked into his eyes. "I may have something for you tonight."

"Torture me all you want, woman. I'll never divulge my secrets until the time is just right," he said. "I will say this, we're going to start looking for a house. Your one bedroom apartment is too tiny and we may crash into each other, although crashing can be fun. Gracie, be mine forever."

"Jarrah, that's the nicest thing I've heard all week."

Chapter Twelve

Four weeks later

The eight girls were back with their families. Two girls were still at Safe Haven. Three of the boys left and hadn't been heard from, and two of the older teenage boys were working on their GEDs.

Jacob and Jonah stayed on at Haven and the older boy wanted to find a way to be made an adult so he could be legal guardian of his younger brother.

Hejazi went down to El Segundo to get his condo put up for sale and packed. He signed papers turning over the presidency of his company to Jack Shore. When he returned to Stockton, he and Grace looked for a house.

Rae was three weeks late with the baby and felt pissed.

By mid-August they'd found a house and Grace couldn't figure out why they needed four bedrooms. When she asked Hejazi about it, he only laughed and whispered it was a secret. That got on her nerves.

The third week of August on a Friday night, Hejazi picked her up from Safe Haven and didn't drive toward her apartment where they were going to stay until the house was ready. When he got onto the freeway heading north, she asked him why they were going to Reno.

He wiggled his eyebrows. "We have a suite reserved at the Atlantis Hotel and we're getting married."

"What? Jarrah we don't have a license yet."

"Yes we do." He pulled an envelope out of his pocket and gave it to her. "I'll need for you to sign it and we'll pick out rings when we get there."

"How did you do this? Wasn't I supposed to be there with you?"

"Have I mentioned that Riley Frost is an amazing attorney?"

Grace smiled. "I'm going to be Grace Hejazi."

"Open the glove box, Babe." He watched her pull out a small flat box. "You said you didn't have any nice jewelry, so I figured no time like the present."

She opened it and saw a solid gold pendant in the shape of a heart with their initials inscribed on it with that day's date.

"Jarrah, this is beautiful." She took it out and put it around her neck. "I guess I can take off my tags now."

"I should have started to spoil you weeks ago." He grinned.

"You do spoil me lots, Cap."

"Grace, love of my life, I have something serious to discuss. You may want me to turn around and go back to Stockton when you hear my plan."

"You're finally going to tell me the big secret?"

"Yeah, I hope you won't be too pissed at me."

She raised her eyebrows and he could see she waited.

"Okay, here goes. I don't like Jacob's idea of applying for emancipation. I think he's too young to get it, anyway, but he did talk to Turner. I'm also afraid the state wouldn't agree to let Jonah stay with him. I'd hate to see them separated."

"Jarrah, what are you thinking?"

"How would you feel about having them stay with us?" He looked at her from the driver's side.

"Four bedrooms. You are a softy, aren't you?"

"When I played checkers with Jonah that first day..." He shook his head. "He was scared and hurting and didn't know who to trust. Shit, if I ever find their mother, I can't guarantee I won't get mean."

She smiled. "I agree with you. Are we just going to foster them or what?"

"To start I thought maybe we could do a guardianship. If we foster them, I'm concerned the system will try to remove them from us, which would screw up any continuity."

"Plus, who knows where they'd end up and if they'd be together."

"Right. What do you think about guardianship first, and then adoption?"

"Instant family."

"Yeah. Jacob would only be with us for three years. Jonah, though, he's only eleven and it kills me that so much has happened to him, but he's still a good kid."

"Jonah has you by the short hairs, doesn't he?"

Hejazi looked at her and laughed. "Yeah, and I'll admit that to no one but you."

"We have some work ahead of us."

"Yep. First things first, let's get married, have a honeymoon for about five minutes and then we can go buy beds and other furniture for the boys."

"When do you want to tell them?"

"Next week, after we talk with Turner and before we get anyone's hopes up."

"Babe, are you ready to make such a huge change in your life? I mean you're laying out some life altering plans here." Grace turned to look directly at him.

"I think so. I'm a little nervous, but I'm pretty sure with your support and intelligence, I'll be all right. I sometimes think too much in the black and white and don't see the gray."

"Then okay. After we pick out the rings, I'm going to need two hours to get ready. Crap, I don't have decent clothes and I don't want to get married in my boots."

"I'm sure the Atlantis Hotel has shops where you can get what you need." He reached over and linked hands with her.

"Yeah, but I'm sure those shops will be expensive."

"You don't get to worry about the price, babe. I'm

pushing to do this the non-traditional way..."

"Yeah, why is it such a rush?" she asked.

Hejazi's heart pounded in his chest. He'd never had a panic attack and thought there was a first time for everything. "Do you want to wait?" He hated how small his voice sounded.

"No, no. I'm just wondering why tonight?"

"When I get an idea, I like to act on it. I hate waiting. I suppose it's a military thing, besides it's already been five weeks."

"It doesn't have anything to do with that woman who broke your heart all those years ago?"

"Huh, you know, I hadn't even thought about it. I suppose it could have something to do with that. I want you to be mine, legally, so no one can steal you away from me."

"Jarrah, no one could do that. I'm stuck on you like ugly and if any woman tries to steal you from me, there will be a pretty big cat fight."

"Period, end of subject?"

"Damn straight."

"Gracie, do you want to wait?"

"No way. You've got me all excited now and I get to buy a dress and have a hot honeymoon with the greatest guy I've ever dated and, hey, I need to buy a fancy, sexy pair of jammies with crotch-less underwear..." Grace continued on, nonstop.

Hejazi laughed so hard tears welled in his eyes. "Babe, stop, stop. You're going to make me crash the car," he howled.

****

They stopped at a jewelry store in Reno that Hejazi had found on-line. Two white-gold wedding bands caught their eye. After saying goodbye to the jeweler, they made their way to the hotel.

Once they were checked in, Grace went to a dress shop and nearly choked at the prices, but Hejazi gave her a credit card to use. She looked and tried on several dresses and finally found a light purple sheath that was only three figures. The material looked thin but wasn't see through.

She then found a shoe store and bought a pair of black sandals with three inch heels and on her way to the elevators realized she'd have to shave her legs. There was a small kiosk that provided razors and other small sundry items.

They didn't have to be to the wedding chapel until eleven o'clock and riding the elevator to their floor, Grace started feeling nervous. She prayed she didn't scrape the hell out of her legs.

After Hejazi got out of the shower, she told him to get dressed and leave the suite. She needed to do some primping and didn't want him to see her before they walked down the aisle. He agreed to meet her in front of the wedding destination.

She showered, washed her hair, and shaved her legs without too much injury. Once out, she dried her hair, put on makeup, and pulled her new lacy panties and bra from the bag. Looking at them, she tossed them to the side and decided all she'd need was the dress and shoes. The light purple looked good with her complexion and when she saw her reflection, realized her nipples could be seen a little, but it didn't matter. The dress would only be on for an hour or so and it was all for Hejazi.

At ten-forty-five she stepped onto the elevator and rode down. She turned a corner and found the chapel. Hejazi stood by the door wearing a black suite with a crisp white shirt and pin-striped black tie. He held a bouquet of cream colored baby rose buds. Looking at him for at least a solid minute, she drank him in. She knew he was the guy she wanted to spend the rest of her life with. She smiled and thought she could get used to playing dress-up from time to time.

Grace watched him look at his watch and then glance around the hallway. He locked eyes with her and walked toward her. She was breathless.

Taking her hand, he started to say something, but stopped. "God Almighty, woman, you are so beautiful! I can hardly breathe."

"I feel the same about you, Jarrah. I'm on fire. You look so handsome."

"Hey, your eyes are almost even with mine." He stepped back and looked at her feet. Nodding, he kissed her hand. "Your legs," he blew out a breath, "I know your legs are great, but wow." He looked blankly at the flowers in his other hand and then laughed. "I feel brainless. I couldn't figure out why I had flowers. These are for you, babe."

"Thank you, they're beautiful. Have we got everything we need?"

"Yep, rings, license, bride and groom. We're good to go. Ready?"

She nodded and he opened the door. They went in, did some paperwork, stood before a guy with big red-hair who called himself Reverend Pat, and said *I do*. Hejazi kissed her, they signed some more papers and walked out the door.

"Thank God that guy didn't look like Elvis," Hejazi said.

"I didn't even think that, but you're right. I never would have kept a straight face if he'd broken out in song."

He held his arm out to her. "Ready for the honeymoon, Mrs. Hejazi?"

"I like the sound of that, the name I mean and the honeymoon." She took his arm.

They stepped onto the elevator holding each other.

"Grace, what if we give your bed to Jacob? My king-sized is coming up next week and then we'll only have to find something for Jonah."

"Jarrah, I love you. The boys haven't even been told our plan yet. What if we wait to see what they want to do first?"

"You're right. I'm putting horses all over the

place, aren't I?"

"Those damn horses can be such trouble."

When the door clicked shut behind them in the suite, Hejazi got a bottle from the small refrigerator. "I got some champagne to celebrate," he said.

"Jarrah, husband, I love you."

"You own my heart, babe." He popped open the bottle of champagne.

A BLAZING DANCE

Chapter Thirteen

Hejazi woke up on his side and tightened his hold around Grace. He moved his face through her hair and wondered what time it could be. It almost caused him to crack up laughing because for the first time in a lot of years he didn't care what the clock said. The only two things he knew for certain was that he felt the happiest he'd ever been and starved for food.

Grace pushed her rear against him and kissed his arm. "Morning, husband or is it afternoon?"

"I'm not sure and find it isn't important. I'm in the most comfortable, happy place I've been in a long time." He heard his cell phone buzz. It was the fourth time it'd gone off in the last half hour.

"Babe, are you going to get that?" she asked.

"If it means letting you go, then no I'm not."

She looked over her shoulder at him. "Jarrah, it could be important."

He kissed her shoulder. "Okay, responsible wife. If it's an advertising call I'll put you over my knee."

She giggled. He flattened onto his back and grabbed the phone. After he'd pushed a couple of buttons, his brows creased.

"It's Jack calling." He sat up and hit the redial button.

"Chief, we've got a problem," Jack said.

"What's up?" He put the phone on speaker so Grace could hear, too.

"Feathertop and his fuckheads made bail yesterday. In the middle of the night they broke into Safe Haven. They took Jacob and a couple of the other boys. When Mrs. Black got the word, she went into labor and Turner took her to the hospital."

"Fuck, we'll be there in two hours." He hung up and looked at Grace. "Babe, sorry, but that's it for the honeymoon."

She threw the sheet off. "Honeymoon part two will be just as great."

Hejazi fumed and couldn't believe those assholes had made bail. They were in the Bronco within a half hour headed south.

He gave his cell-phone to Grace and directed her with a number he wanted called. She got Henry Tanado from the FBI onto the speaker.

"Henry, what the fuck happened? How did Feathertop get bail money?" Hejazi asked.

"Not sure who paid. We thought there was enough proof to get bail rejected, but the asshole judge didn't see him as a threat. The girls being locked up in the cages made no difference."

"He took three of the boys from Haven. How is that not a threat? Haven is a sanctuary," he shouted.

"I know that, man. We're working on it, but they haven't returned to the warehouse. We're following up on leads and talking to the other kids to see if they know where they might have gone."

"Henry, I gave Jacob a cell phone," he recited the number. "Can you get your electronic geeks to start tracing the GPS card?"

"I'm on it. I'll get back to you."

Grace turned the phone off and crossed her arms. "Jarrah..."

"Grace..."

They spoke at the same time.

"You go first, babe," she said.

"I talked to Jacob about what happened to him. The poor kid thought he'd done something wrong. He was confused and we worked with Haven's therapist. I swear to God if any of those fucks touch him again I will have to kill them."

Grace reached between the seats and pulled her Glock out of her bag. "I'm right there with you, husband."

"Wife, I love you."

"That's a good thing, because if anything with this goes sideways we may have a lot to explain. Love you, too."

When they pulled up in front of Safe Haven, Hejazi saw Jonah sitting on the steps. He parked the Bronco on the street in front and got out. The boy ran to him and flew into his arms.

"They took him, Mr. Hejazi. They took Jacob," the boy said. "Jake tried to fight just like you taught us, but he wasn't strong enough and they knocked him out."

Hejazi looked at the kid and saw a red mark on his cheek. "What happened to your face?" He put the boy on his feet.

"I tried to fight, too, but one of Feathertop's men hit me and I landed on my ass."

"You did good, Jonah. We need to get some ice on that."

They started to move into the building when Hejazi's cell phone went off again. Grace pulled it out of her pocket and looked at the screen. He saw her eyebrows fold.

"It's a text from Jacob. He says he doesn't know where he is, but it smells like fertilizer. Jarrah, there are a couple of plants down at the waterfront."

"We need a map. I'll get ice and you get your computer up and running."

They walked into the lobby and found six of his men standing around.

"How'd you guys get here so fast?"

"Jack called us. Griggsy got the chopper going. He's an ace pilot, you know?" Jonesy said.

He turned to Grace. "Can you get the ice, babe, and then start the computer? Jonah you go with her. I'll be right up." He looked at the desk where someone always sat, but it was empty.

"Haven's guard, Lawson, got shot. He's in surgery at the hospital." Rand looked up as Grace stopped on the stairs. "He'll be okay. The doctor didn't think the bullet hit anything important."

She nodded and continued up with Jonah following.

Hejazi turned to his men. "Guys, this is going to be messy and I may be asking you to do something that might make you want to back out. When we find these guys, I'm not sure I want any of them left breathing."

"Chief, two of the boys went of their own free will. Jacob was taken. Our mission is to rescue one boy. If I'm threatened or any of my teammates or the kid, I'll be ready to threaten back." Griggs said and the rest of the men nodded.

"No holding back, Chief," Rand said.

"No holding back," the men all said together.

Hejazi nodded. "You guys are going to get a big bonus for this one."

"You know we'll hold you to that?" Griggs laughed.

"I expect nothing less."

After they got the locations of the fertilizer plants and descriptions of the surrounding area, they checked their weapons and loaded the vehicles. FBI Agent Tanado called Hejazi and reported that the GPS on Jacob's cell phone registered to one particular plant.

They looked at the layout of the building and formulated a plan.

Hejazi pulled Grace into the office were they'd kissed all those weeks ago. He hugged her tightly.

"Babe, I want you to stay here," he said.

She pushed back. "Why?"

He put his hand on her cheek. "This could get ugly and I don't want you involved."

"Jarrah..."

"Listen, with Rae in the hospital Haven needs you here. Jonah needs you here and trusts you. If things go south he may need you even more. And, I'd feel better if you're in a safe place." He looked at her beautiful green eyes and wanted to be able to assure her that everything would be fine, but she was smart and knew the reality of the situation.

"Jarrah, you better come back to me in one piece."

He put his forehead against hers. "I hear you, wife. I love you." He framed her face with his hands. "You are my life now."

She reached behind her back and pulled out her Glock. "There are twelve shots in the clip and one in the chamber." She took another clip out of her pocket. "Here's twelve more. Take it for luck."

He smiled and pulled out his Smith and Wesson. "Hold this for me. It's been with me for a long time."

They exchanged guns and then he kissed her and when he pulled back her green eyes looked up at him with confidence.

"Go kick some ass, Cap, and tell Feathertop his balls are safe since I'm not there."

"Who says they're safe?" He kissed her again and then left the office.

As he and his men pulled away from the sidewalk he saw Grace and Jonah standing at the entrance to Safe Haven.

Chapter Fourteen

Hejazi parked his SUV on the street down from the plant and looked at the building through binoculars.

"Anybody see movement?"

"Negative, Chief. It's a big fucking building," one of the men reported.

"We're going to take the action inside," he said. He lowered the binoculars and thought. When they'd taken Feathertop the first time, the creep had eight guards with him. Would he have the same numbers or more?

"Jack, give us the lay out."

"The main floor is processing equipment, and storage. At the south end, second level, are offices, a cafeteria and a locker room."

"Griggsy, any way for you to get on top?"

"Yep, there's a fire escape ladder in back. Want me up?"

"Roger that. Before we move in, I'd feel more comfortable knowing what we're facing and the count of opposition."

The men waited for a report from Griggs. After a couple of minutes he was on the roof and found airvents.

"Along the north inside, there's a stairwell up to the second floor. Two guards at the bottom. One holding an AK rapid fire and the other guy...shit...looks like an AK-103."

"All teams meet at the south end." He got out of the Bronco. After he pulled a semi-automatic from the back, he ran across the lot and met the men at a chain link fence. With the gun slung over his shoulder, he held Grace's Glock in his big hand and watched as Jones cut the fence. They moved to a back door.

"Griggsy, we're at the southeast corner door. Can you see anyone?"

"Hold. I need to move down."

They waited and knew the man on the roof needed to find an air vent he could see through.

"Chief, you've got one guard at the door. Want him out?"

"Do you have a silencer?"

"Affirmative."

Hejazi thought a minute and felt on the fence. If they took this step what would it mean for his crew?

"Chief, are you riding the fence on this one? Remember what those fucks did to those kids," he heard Griggs.

"Roger, clear the door and then take out the two on the stairs. Let us know if you see any other movement."

"Roger that." After thirty seconds Griggs said,

"Ground floor clear. No movement."

Jones used a crowbar to get the door opened and all six walked in, each taking up a position.

Hejazi knew he went over the top, but he felt a strong concern that Jacob could be in terrible peril, and not only that, but his anger was also at a breaking point. They moved through the ground floor in increments to the stairs and walked past the two bodies. They collected the guns and extra clips and started to the second floor. Halfway up, a shot rang out and a bullet hit the wall above them as a body fell forward at the top floor landing.

"Thanks Griggsy," one man whispered.

"Chief, you've got three waiting at the top. Featherfuck has Jacob in the hall behind the three. He's got a knife to the kid's throat."

Hejazi took the rest of the stairs two at a time. When he turned the corner, he stopped. The three men all held AK's pointed at him. He held Grace's gun level and pointed straight at the old man.

"Let Jacob go," he snarled.

"Mr. Hejazi, it would seem we're at a standoff."

"No, fuckhead, you aren't getting out of this one. The FBI have the building surrounded."

Hejazi knew the agents were on their way from Sacramento, but he felt sure they hadn't arrived, just yet. He didn't give a shit that he'd just told a bald-face-lie.

He looked directly at Jacob. "Thanks for the text

message, kid. We were able to track you from that. Good job." Hejazi smiled. He knew he held the advantage in his pocket even with guns pointed at him. He glanced quickly to his left and right and then looked at Feathertop's men. His team was positioned perfectly. "You guys have fifteen seconds to clear out," he said to the guards.

"You're full of yourself, aren't you, Mr. Hejazi? We've already been freed once. It will happen again."

"Griggsy, *vicis est iam, iuguolo him*," he said and continue to smile.

"What's that gibberish? Some sort of Arab language?" Feathertop sneered.

"No, it's Latin, asshole."

Griggs swung down through the air vent and shot the old man in the back of his head. Feathertop died instantly and fell forward on top of Jacob. At the same time, Hejazi and his men fired on the three others, but only injured them. The AK's landed on the floor as the men clutched at their arms and legs.

He put the Glock into his holster and stepped over the men on the floor. As he pushed Feathertop off of Jacob, the kid stared up at him.

"Hey boy-o, ready to get out of here?" Hejazi put his hand out.

The kid grabbed it and got pulled up. "Yes, sir."

He saw a streak on the kid's neck and realized he bled. "Anyone here have the first aid kit?"

"It's in the Bronco, but I have this." Rand took a

handkerchief from his pocket.

Hejazi put the piece of fabric up to Jacob's neck just as Griggs came down from the ceiling feet first. He looked at his boss.

"Latin? Really? Are you trying to give me a headache?" Griggs chided.

"What? Did you forget your training?" Hejazi answered as he helped Jacob get over the old man's body.

"Yeah, but in the heat of the moment I need longer than fifteen seconds and a Universal Translator would have helped, too." Griggs walked toward the other men.

Hejazi looked at Jacob. He took a pocketknife out. "Let's see about getting those ropes off your wrists. How the hell did you text me?"

Jacob held his hands up and wiggled his fingers. "My phone is in the pocket on the side of my leg. If they'd tied my hands behind my back it wouldn't have worked. All I had to do was reach down."

"Jake, you are one smart kid, do you know that?"

Jacob grabbed Hejazi's hand and shook it. He saw the kid's eyes well.

"Thank you, again, sir," he croaked.

Hejazi put his hands on the boy's shoulders. "Anytime, Jacob," he said and pulled him into a tight hug.

"Am I going to go to jail?"

He moved the kid back. "Why on earth would you

think that?"

"Feathertop's body and all the picks I did. I can't go to jail. There won't be anyone to look after Jonah."

"Jake, that asshole held a knife to your throat and my team's only thought was getting you safe. You're not to blame yourself or feel guilty. He treated you badly, threatened to cut your neck and got what he deserved. Although, I can think of worse..." He looked at the kid's brown eyes. "Never mind, let's get you out of here. I know the Feds will want to question you, but you're not answering anything without a lawyer present."

"If it's not my fault, why do I need an attorney?"

"It's not about this. I don't want them dragging you or Jonah off to Child Protective Services." As they went down the stairs, Hejazi put his arm around Jacob's shoulders. "Do you know what happened to the other two boys that left Safe Haven?"

"No. They knocked me out and when I woke up, I was alone."

"Okay. We'll let the feds know that."

After a very long night of being questioned and recorded by the FBI, Hejazi found Grace in the kitchen on the top floor. She turned and saw him in the doorway.

"Hey." She put a towel down and walked up to him. "You look exhausted."

"Yeah, someone kept me awake most of last

night."

"Yep, I'm needy and want more."

"Me, too. I promise we'll have a decent honeymoon once everything settles down." He wrapped his arms around her. "Where are the boys? Turner approached me about signing the Guardianship papers this evening. We need to talk to them first."

"Yeah, but don't you want to get some rest?"

"No. After what Jake went through, I want him to know he's cared for and will have a place to call home."

"Jarrah, you have the biggest heart." She put her hands around his neck and gave him a kiss.

They walked to the stairs and went down to the boys' floor. Grace smiled up at him. "Did Turner tell you Rae gave birth to a girl this afternoon?"

"Yeah, how sweet is that?" He knocked on the boys' door.

Grace opened it and they walked in. Jacob sat on one bed with his sketch pad and Jonah lay on his stomach reading a comic book.

"Hey guys, do you have a minute?" Hejazi asked.

Jonah moved to the edge of his bed and Hejazi sat next to him.

"What's going on?" Jacob put his sketch pad aside.

"Grace and I have an issue we want to talk to you about."

Grace sat next to Jacob.

"What kind of issues?" Jacob said.

Hejazi pushed back and leaned against the wall. "We have a proposal for you."

"What's a proposal?" Jonah asked and pushed back next to Hejazi.

"It's a plan and sort of an offer." Grace smiled and wrapped her hand around Jacob's arm. "You see, Grace and I got married last night and have bought a house. Our proposal is for you two to come live with us." Hejazi looked at both boys.

Jonah smiled, but Jacob frowned. "For how long would we live with you?" he asked.

"I guess until you do something stupid like go off to college or get married," Hejazi said.

"Hey, mister. Getting married isn't stupid. It was your idea anyway." Grace smirked.

Hejazi crossed his eyes. "The point here is we'd be your legal guardians until you reach eighteen. After that you can do what you like."

"Does that mean you'd adopt us?" Jonah leaned on his arm.

"That's something we could talk about. We'd be your guardians to start, and before you decide, you should know there will be rules to follow. Grace and I are pretty easy going, but we're both ex-Marines and go by the book."

"Jake, we wouldn't have to live in the car or run off like we did when Mom got into trouble," Jonah said.

"What if we don't like it?" Jacob still frowned.

"We'd figure something else out. It can't hurt to try, right?" Grace said.

"I guess we could try it."

"Good. Now we've got some things at the house to get done. How about we say move in on Wednesday? Tomorrow, I want you two dressed and ready to go by eight o'clock. There's a lot to do at the house and we'll need to hit Home Depot for paint and ladders and yard equipment. We've got to get the house in shape by Wednesday."

"I'll be ready." Jonah grinned.

Chapter Fifteen

One month later - September

Grace looked at Hejazi and knew he was close to the breaking point.

"Mr. Hejazi, I'm afraid you don't understand me. Tenth graders only have one optional class. If Jacob would like to give up the woodworking class for art he can do that."

"Mr. Pinder, I don't see why he has to take PE. He's not an athletic kid."

"For boys like him, it's best if they have an outlet for their aggression. It makes them easier to deal with."

"Deal with? Jacob doesn't *need* to be dealt with, Pinder."

Grace put her hand on Hejazi's arm. "Mr. Pinder, could you excuse us. I need to speak with my husband." She stood and pulled on Hejazi's arm. When the office door closed, she looked up at him.

"That man is a prick," he snarled.

"I agree with you one-hundred percent, babe. The Nazi-principle is a dick, but if Jake's going to this school we need to work with them. You can't pull out your Smith and Wesson."

"Do you have something in mind?"

"I do and it would only be a little lie, but I know a

doctor that would back us. Just follow my lead, okay?" They went back into the office and sat down.

"Mr. Pinder, I'm sorry about the misunderstanding. There is a reason that Jacob can't take physical education. We didn't want everyone to know because it embarrasses him, but I think we can trust you." She looked at Hejazi and took his hand. "Jacob has asthma. When he gets overtaxed his attacks can become so bad that...well, I'd hate for the PE teachers to have to call 9-1-1 multiple times."

"Asthma?" The principal's face pinched.

"Oh yes, it's very scary and I'm sure his doctor would be willing to send a note to your school nurse."

"I'm sure."

****

They walked to the Bronco and Hejazi smiled. "My wife is the most brilliant woman on the planet. I'm the luckiest guy," he sang and shook his hips when they stopped to let a car go by.

"That was easy." She took his hand. "If we have to deal with the Nazi principal for the next three years we'll have to remember Jacob has asthma."

"I'm going to defer all Nazi dealings to you from now on."

When they walked into the house Jacob appeared in the kitchen. Hejazi walked over and put his hand on the kid's shoulder trying not to smile.

"How'd it go?" Jacob looked from one to the

other.

"It would seem you'll be taking woodworking and art class this year. Screw PE"

"Yes!" Jacob jumped up and pumped his fist. "Thank you, this is great. I talked to one of the older kids down the street who said Mr. Howard is a great teacher."

Hejazi arched his eyebrow. "You owe me."

"What?" Jacob stopped jumping.

"Put your shoes on and let's go trim some hedges. Then we'll all go for pizza and stop at Wally World to get school supplies."

"Deal. I'll be right back."

He felt Grace's hands move around his waist and pulled her in front of him.

"You are making a great dad."

"You mean despite wanting to kill the principal, I'm still a great dad candidate?" He nibbled her bottom lip.

"I'd vote for you."

He kissed her, swatted her rear, and moved to the garage door. "Tell Jake I'm outside."

"Yes, Captain."

He turned and heard a double set of footfalls coming down the stairs. He tilted his head. "Ah, our thundering herd. I guess it's good we sort of like them."

The brothers walked into the garage and he gave them rakes and buckets. They went into the back yard and spent the afternoon working side by side. Hejazi loved these days.

Three months later - The evening before Thanksgiving

Grace stood in the kitchen and finished making a batch of cranberry relish. She put some into a small bowl and grabbed three spoons.

In the living room her boys sat in their usual positions, Hejazi stretched out in the recliner with his laptop open, Jacob on the couch with his sketch pad, and Jonah on his back on the floor. He read aloud from his current book. Hejazi took over helping with homework and discovered Jonah's reading abilities were below the level for his age. They'd started going to the public library and picked out some books. Jonah then read them out loud to Hejazi and his levels picked up in just two months. Grace sat on the arm of the recliner and listened to the story.

"Cassie threw off her shoes and jumped on the unicorn's back." Jonah sat up. "This is stupid."

Hejazi closed his laptop. Grace felt his hand on the middle of her back.

"Why is it stupid?" he asked Jonah.

"Everybody knows that some guy saw a rhinoceros in Africa and made up the stories about unicorns. They're not real."

"Did you Goggle that?" He pushed the footrest down and sat up.

"Yeah."

"What was the guy's name who saw the rhinoceros?"

"I don't know. He just did."

"We'll Google it again tonight. I want to know this guy's name and why he made up the stories."

Jonah stared at him. "Weird."

"Sweetheart, what's the stuff in the dish?" He looked up at Grace.

"It's homemade cranberry relish for tomorrow. I need volunteer taste testers." She waved a spoon.

"I'm in." Hejazi smiled.

She scooped some up and fed him. "You can tell me if it's too tart."

He chewed. "That is good. Wow, honey, can I have some more?" He held his mouth open.

She looked at the boys. "I brought spoons for you guys, too. Want a taste?"

Jonah popped up off the floor. He scooped up a little and his lips puckered. "It's sour, like Sweet Tarts," he stuck out his tongue.

She looked at Jacob and held up the last spoon. "You know you want to try it."

He laughed and came over. "Wow, it's good, but Jonah's right its sour."

"Hmm...maybe it needs a little more sugar. I'll sweeten it up a bit."

Hejazi sat back in the chair. "Jake, how's your art class going? You haven't said much."

"It's good." He sat back on the couch. "Mr. Howard likes my idea of a comic book about street kids. That's what I'm working on for the next six weeks."

"That's great. I think maybe we could get it published after it's finished for school."

"Really? That would be cool."

"Can I ask a question?" Jonah flopped back onto the floor.

Grace and Hejazi waited for the boy to formulate his question.

"Last night at dinner when Grace said she was going to have a baby, I just wondered what would happen to me and Jake."

"Jonah!" Jake said scowling.

"No, that's a good question, Jake. As far as we're concerned nothing will happen with you. You've become a part of our family," Hejazi said.

"Jonah." Grace set the bowl and spoons aside and sat on the floor next to the boy. She put her arm around him. "We love you guys. You're here for good."

"But we're not your ballogical kids." Jonah looked up at her.

"What?"

"I can't say that word right. We're not your real kids. Your baby will be yours."

"Sweetheart, you and Jake are going to be big brothers. It's a big responsibility being a brother and he or she will need you very much."

"For how long?" Jake asked from the couch.

"As far as I know, forever." Hejazi arched his eyebrows. "Riley will have the adoption papers ready to go in a couple of weeks and I can't think of a better Christmas present. I told you a while back, you're with us until you turn eighteen or go to college. We hope you'll be a part of this family for a long time, okay?"

"What if our mom comes back?" Jonah asked.

Grace wanted to die. The child welfare authorities found their mom who signed off her parental rights. They hadn't told the boys yet and it broke her heart.

"If your mother shows up, we'll see where we stand." Hejazi looked at her and she knew he found this a difficult situation.

Jonah leaned against her and she heard him whisper, "Okay."

"Boys, the most important thing for Jarrah and me is that you are happy and safe. We want you to have all the advantages available in life." She felt her throat tighten and knew she was having a hormone surge. "You guys are very important to us." She wiped her cheek and Jonah hugged her.

Hejazi looked at Jacob. "Are we okay for now?"

Jacob nodded.

Grace saw Jonah look at his brother and smiled nodding like a bobble headed doll.

"Dad, can we go to the craft store this weekend? Some of my pens are drying up," Jacob said and looked at Hejazi.

Grace saw the stunned expression on her husband's face.

"What did you call me?"

Jacob clasped his hands between his knees. "Dad?"

"We talked about it last week and decided to call you guys Mom and Dad, I mean if it's okay," Jonah said.

Grace watched Hejazi. She saw his eyes well up and he swallowed a couple of times. "Boys." He turned his head and closed his eyes for a second, then looked at Jacob. "I'd be very honored if you called me Dad."

Jonah looked up at Grace. "Hi, Mom."

She laughed and hugged him. "Hi." A couple of tears rolled down her cheeks.

Hejazi wiped his eyes. "I don't know about anyone else, but I need some ice cream and maybe a tough game of Rummy."

"Cool." Jonah stood up.

"Jonah, get the deck of cards from the top drawer of my desk. Jacob, go and clean off the table." Hejazi got up from the recliner.

The boys moved and he offered Grace a hand up off the floor. He wrapped his arms around her and put his head on her shoulder.

"Are you okay, babe?" She heard him sniff.

"The boys constantly surprise me."

She pulled back and smiled. "We've been pretty lucky, you know?"

He put his hand on her cheek and gave her a quick kiss. "I waited a long time for this kind of feeling and sometimes I don't know if I'm coming or going."

"We have learned a lot."

He kissed her nose. "You got that right. They're going to wear me out."

"Rummy only to five-hundred points tonight, I'm tired."

"Good thinking. I love you, wife."

"Back at you times ten.

****

Hejazi stared at the ceiling and listened to Grace's even breaths. His brain thought over the last five months and how so many things in his life had changed.

He'd been single for so long. He thought having a pregnant wife and two boys calling him Dad should make him anxious, but he found that a soothing pulse ran through his system.

Grace rolled onto her side. "Babe, you're dithering. What's wrong?"

"Not a thing in the world. I was just thinking I'd better call my folks in the morning and let them know you're pregnant. You need to call yours, too."

"Yeah, I just wanted a day or two before the grandmother's start calling with suggestions."

He chuckled. "Yeah, I can hear it now. Only babies should have goat's milk and no disposable diapers, they are very bad," he said using a middle-eastern accent. "That will be from my grandma. She drove my mom nuts."

Grace propped up on her elbow. "The boys really got to you earlier."

"Yeah, they did, but in a good way. I wish this would have happened earlier in my life, but then I'm glad I waited. And then I wished we'd gotten Jonah and Jake when they were younger so we'd have had them longer."

"We'll work with the time we have, and I've thought that, too. When Jonah said they wouldn't have to live in the car again, it stabbed my heart. Jarrah, we need to tell them about their mom."

"I know. Let's wait until after the holidays." He turned and looked at the clock. "Wife, I have an idea." He sat up and got out of bed. "Get up and put on something warm." He opened his drawer and pulled out a pair of sweats. "Come on, beautiful. This will be fun."

"Jarrah, it's eleven-thirty. What are you doing?" She went to her side of the chest of drawers and put on a pair of fleece pajamas.

"Let's camp out in the backyard and sleep under the stars tonight. Us and the boys."

"Babe, we don't have any camping equipment."

"I know, but we have that big old king-sized quilt and pillows and extra blankets. We'll keep each other warm. I'm going to get the boys." He walked down the hall and went into both rooms to wake up Jonah and Jacob. He told them to put on sweats and socks and bring their pillows out to the backyard.

He pulled the quilt and extra blankets out of a hall closet and headed down the stairs. After he'd spread the quilt on the ground, he turned and saw his family staring at him. He smiled. "These will be the days in the future when you talk about the crazy old man who made you camp out in the backyard in the late fall."

"You want us to sleep out here?" Jacob asked.

"Yep, we'll crash under the stars. We have each other to keep us warm."

"We've never been camping before," Jonah said.

"Yes, we have. All those nights in the car were just like it." Jacob answered.

"Sleeping in the car doesn't count."

"Sure it does, but the only good part was if it was raining at least we could stay dry." Jacob shook his head.

Jonah walked onto the quilt and looked up at Hejazi. "Where are you going to sleep, Dad?"

"If we break the quilt into quarters, I'll park here." He threw his pillow down in the middle.

"I'm here then." Jonah was next to Hejazi.

He looked at Grace. "Sweetheart, next to me or between the boys?"

She turned to Jacob. "I'm going to sleep next to Dad. He is very warm at night and I don't want to freeze my butt off."

They all got down on the ground, lay on their backs and looked up at the clear night sky. Hejazi brought out extra blankets and before long they were spread out over them.

"Guys, see that cluster of stars right there, that looks like a bow. Look to the left and you see the three stars that line up?"

"Yeah," Jonah said.

"That's called Orion's Belt."

"Wow, he doesn't have a belt buckle," Jonah snickered.

The comment struck him funny and he laughed. "You're right. I guess his pants should fall down."

"What's that one over there?" Jonah pointed.

Hejazi enjoyed this and felt great that the boys seemed interested. He wasn't sure if they were just playing him, but thought if he could show them something simple, they might become more comfortable. He glanced over at Grace and saw she'd fallen asleep. He quieted the boys, but they continued to look at the stars.

Jacob sat up and looked over Hejazi at Grace. "Dad, what do you think we should get Mom for Christmas?"

"Yeah." Jonah said.

"That's a good question." Hejazi hadn't thought about Christmas with all the other things that came his way in the last months. "We'll have to think about it. I know she doesn't have a lot of jewelry. We'll have to go shopping and have a look."

"Maybe she'd like a puppy," Jonah said.

Hejazi put his arm behind his head and almost

laughed. "That's a thought, but you know she'll have the baby to take care of, maybe that would be too much right now."

"We could get her stuff for the nursery, or maybe I could design something for the walls in the baby's room. Something I could paint," Jacob said.

"That's a good idea, too, but right now I think we need to get some sleep." He saw Jacob lay back down and after a bit the boys were sawing logs.

Hejazi looked up at the stars and realized that due to the fact that he and Grace had come together so quickly, bought a house, and adopted the boys, he'd not been able to really get to know them and had some work to do. This was in his wheelhouse and he could make it work.

Chapter Sixteen

Six months later

Hejazi walked down a grocery store aisle and stopped in the pickle section. He tried to find the exact sweet pickles that Grace craved. They had one more month before the baby would arrive and with her blood pressure being high, he did everything he could to keep her happy. Today it was sweet pickles and only a certain brand.

The pieces fell together nicely over the past months. With Riley's help, the legal adoptions of the two boys went through just before Christmas. Hejazi finally told them about their mother giving up her rights. Jacob and Jonah seemed hurt by the news and the eleven year old, Jonah, cried in Grace's arms. They wanted to be honest with the boys and after they'd had a couple of sessions with a therapist, Jacob and Jonah realized it wasn't their fault. Now the Hejazi's wanted them and that's all that mattered.

He found the jar of pickles on the shelf and felt his cell phone vibrate just as he picked them out. He lifted the phone out of his pocket and saw Jonah called.

"Hey, boy-o. What's up?"

"Dad, you need to come home right now," the kid said, breathing hard. "Somebody shot Mom."

Hejazi dropped the jar of pickles, left the cart in the aisle and hurried to the exit of the store. He took long strides and tried to keep from running into other people.

"Tell me what happened, son?"

"I'm not sure. Jacob said he heard Mom talking to someone in the kitchen. I saw him, some bald guy and then I heard the shot."

Hejazi stopped at the door of the Bronco. "Jonah, your Mom..."

"She's alive, Dad, but the baby is kicking. Jacob's on the phone with 9-1-1. Wait a minute, Mom wants to talk to you."

He opened the SUV and climbed in.

"Jarrah?" She sounded out of breath.

"Baby, hold on. I'm on my way."

"No. Listen, remember the case you told me about when Sophie Frost's dad tried to kill her. Wasn't there some bald guy involved?"

"Yeah, Booth."

"That's it. He said his name was Booth and kept repeating, *what goes around comes around and it's now time to pay the piper.*"

"Gracie, you don't sound so good." He knew he was breaking the law being on his cell phone while driving, but he didn't give a shit.

"The shot hit my lung and I'm having a hard time breathing. My water broke, Jarrah. I think the baby is going to be early. I love you, sweetheart."

"I love you, too, Grace. Hold on, I'll be..."

He heard the phone drop.

Read the First in the Series

Taking Risks

Book 1 in the Dicey Dance Series

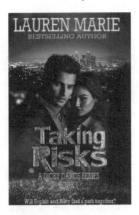

Riley Frost is an attorney who was once a Dom and liked control. He left the life style and tried to figure out what he wanted in his life. He'd never found a woman with a sense of adventure and passion, until one night when he walked into a bar and...

Sophie Pantagen is the vice-president of her father's company. She's spent the past ten years having one-off's with men who are strangers. She never found out their names and didn't care to see them ever again. That was until one night in a bar when she met...

Riley and Sophie find each other at a time when both are looking for more in life. They're not sure what it is they want, but think they may have found it.

Sophie's father is a cut-throat business man and when he thinks she has turned traitor to the company, he comes after her with vengeance. When the lies and deceit from her father's past are brought to Sophie's attention she feels lost and isn't sure what road to choose.

Will Sophie and Riley find a path together?

Lauren Marie lives in Western Washington State with her calico cat – Shiva. She is a member of the Writers Cooperative of Pacific Northwest

Going to Another Place - revised edition released 2018

One Touch at Cobb's Bar and Grill - Montana Ranch series, short story

Taking Risks- Book 1 The Dicey Dance Series

A Lost Life- The Dicey Dance Series Book 2

Loves Touch - Then and Now

Love's Embers - Canon City series book 1

Love on Ice - Canon City series book 2

Big Mike, Little Mike - short story

The Haller Lake series - A Demon Scheme

The Haller Lake series 2 - Magick's Pathway

The Haller Lake series 3 - Portal Hop

Secrets Beyond Dreams

Laura's Choice - 2019

Golden Ribbons – revised edition -2020

Lie in Our Grave – Her Lie book 3 - 2019

Cursed Through Time -2021

Lost in Confusion – 2021

Lost in Confusion 2 – Streaming Stalker – 2022

Lost in Confusion 3 – A New Life - 2022

Love in the Morning Mist – Canon City series book 3 – 2022

Love's Touch Then and Now – 2nd edition 2022

Three Lost Men – Lost in Confusion book 4 – 2023

The Haller Lake series 4 – Dancing Flames at Haller Lake – 2024

Books to Go Now

You can find more stories such as this at www.bookstogonow.com

If you enjoy this Books to Go Now story please leave a review for the author on a review site which you purchased the eBook. Thanks!

We pride ourselves with representing great stories at low prices. We want to take you into the digital age offering a market that will allow you to grow along with us in our journey through the new frontier of digital publishing.
Some of our favorite award-winning authors have now joined us. We welcome readers and writers into our community.

We want to make sure that as a reader you are supplied with never-ending great stories. As a company, Books to Go Now, wants its readers and writers supplied with positive experience and encouragement so they will return again and again.

   We want to hear from you. Our readers and writers are the cornerstone of our company. If there is something you would like to say or a genre that you would like to see, please email us at bookstogonow@bookstogonow.com

Made in United States
Troutdale, OR
12/01/2024

25422546R00076